ONE IN A

Million

ONE IN A
Million

Christine Marie Blai

iUniverse®

ONE IN A MILLION

This is a work of fiction. All of the characters, names, incidents, organizations, and dialogue in this novel are either the products of the author's imagination or are used fictitiously.

iUniverse books may be ordered through booksellers or by contacting:

iUniverse
1663 Liberty Drive
Bloomington, IN 47403
www.iuniverse.com
1-800-Authors (1-800-288-4677)

ISBN: 978-1-5320-0227-4 (sc)
ISBN: 978-1-5320-0228-1 (e)

Library of Congress Control Number: 2016911433

Print information available on the last page.

iUniverse rev. date: 08/09/2016

Chapter 1

It was the most beautiful city in the world. That's what the San Francisco Tourist and Visitors Bureau touted. And maybe they were right. But in the ten days since Mariette Stuart had arrived, what she saw most was the view from her hotel-room window. She had to do something quick. There were only four days left. She couldn't very well go back to Ohio saying all she did was saunter through two of the nine galleries in the de Young Museum and the Asian Art Museum before wandering out the door, spend an entire day riding the carousel and eating corn dogs in Golden Gate Park, and travel all the way out to Lincoln Park to stare back at Rodin's *The Thinker* at the entrance to the California Palace of the Legion of Honor and never go inside. Today was going to be different. Today, she would accomplish something. She could feel it.

Standing in her hotel room, Mariette sorted through her clothes in the open suitcase on the bed. The green tweed jumper matched with hunter-green tights and brown leather clogs was her favorite outfit. Wearing that would make her feel good. Maybe it would even motivate her. The twenty-four-year-old student slipped it on and stood in front of the mirror. As her deep green eyes watched her fingers tousle through her short black curls, Mariette boldly decided to take a stab at touring the downtown Civic Center.

The formal garden at the heart of the center was Mariette's first destination. Meandering the walkways, she heeded the flowers and trees, fountain and flags. That swiftly accomplished, the buildings surrounding the garden were her next order of business. She started with the largest one, San Francisco City Hall. There she hooked up with a tour. The guide immediately started listing the tons of granite and marble that went into the "Baroque masterpiece that was modeled after but stood higher than the Capitol Building in Washington, DC."

As the others looked up to the huge dome, Mariette watched her clogs on the shiny marble floor. The group was herded into an elevator to visit a courtroom and maybe even meet the mayor. She was not in the mood for hearing statistics, visiting courtrooms, or meeting politicians. Letting the others file past, Mariette waited until the elevator doors closed and made a beeline to the revolving glass doors.

Mariette breathed a sigh of relief as she walked past the guard, twirled through the doors, and ran down the steps of city hall. Once outside, she immediately chided herself. Mariette was on vacation. She was supposed to be seeing the sights. She was supposed to be absorbing some culture. She was supposed to be having a good time.

A group of women debarked a bus at the end of the block. Mariette ran to catch the tail end of what she assumed was another tour. Swept along with the crowd, she was ushered into the Civic Center Auditorium. Symphony schedules and calendars and the yearly report were thrust into her hands. The strange assortment of pamphlets befuddled Mariette. She looked around the auditorium. Slides of musical instruments, dead composers, and sheet music flashed erratically on portable movie screens. Old pictures of dour men in formal dress scowled at her from makeshift partitions labeled "Your Conductors 1911–Present."

Mariette sat down on a metal folding chair to decipher the literature in her hands and make some sense of the assemblage. Immediately, a woman seated across the table from her started drilling Mariette on proper form-filling and telephone-answering techniques. She was in the middle of a recruitment drive for symphony-worker volunteers! The women had been performed to and fed. Now it was time, once again, to volunteer their services for the upcoming season. Typing, telephoning, and ticket selling were all needed. Symphony executives, musicians, and even the music director were on hand to convince the women the contribution of their services was vital.

Mariette shook her head at her own rashness. There was nothing of interest for her here. She wasn't staying in San Francisco. She knew nothing of symphonic music. She started to leave.

Heading toward the exit, Mariette was caught in a crush of women. The women pushed and shouted questions toward the core of the circle as they huddled. Mariette tried forcing herself through the barrage, but the circle wouldn't give; it only tightened. Repeatedly, she was shoved inward. The more Mariette tried to wriggle through the crowd, the more she was pushed toward its core. Digging her elbows into her side and her fists to her chest, Mariette expended one last-ditch effort to propel herself through. Instead, she was spun around, coming face-to-face with the crowd's object of attention.

The "object" the women were outdoing themselves for was a man, an absurdly good-looking man. He appeared to be in his thirties. Dressed in a dark blue pin-striped business suit, he was calm and very much at ease. His polish and presence indicated his rightfulness in the middle of things. Wedged into her spot and trying not to be shoved any farther forward, Mariette surveyed the man.

He stood a head above her. His light brown hair was medium length, meticulously cut, and carelessly tossed back from his brow. High, prominent cheekbones melded into a long face with a solid chin. The face was compelling and masculine. And despite the sober expression he held, she thought his mouth quite sensual. But it was his eyes—his all-seeing gray eyes with one eyebrow not quite matching the other—that piqued Mariette's interest. She watched as he fielded questions while impassively observing the crowd.

One florid woman in a tight cashmere sweater waved, hand held high over her head, and said, "Don't you think Chopin is the greatest master of keyboard counterpoint since Bach?"

"Undoubtedly." The man's face remained stoic, his eyes serious.

"Who's your favorite composer?" queried the tiny blonde woman next to her.

"Beethoven."

"He's the one you won the Leeds Piano Competition with," a woman in a tennis dress and turban informed him. Turning to her neighbor, she proclaimed, "We saw him win it in Budapest five years ago. He was marvelous."

"No, no, Colly," her friend said. "Budapest is the Liszt. The Leeds is in Yorkshire." She turned to the beleaguered man. "Isn't that right, Christian?"

Mariette watched in stunned amazement as the women shamelessly flaunted and flirted for the man. They were reminiscent of the girls in her dormitory back home. She could never figure out whether women behaved like that to impress one another or the man. She found the women's actions embarrassing, but the man's reaction kept intriguing

Mariette. He paid solemn attention to the women, giving them the impression that their questions were astute. In return, he fed back what they had just said while adding very little of his own.

"I did play some Beethoven selections for the Leeds."

Mariette found the questions getting sillier, but not once did the man show anything other than solemn, rapt attention.

An eccentric-looking woman in layers of flowered cloth was next. She twirled her finger through a well-worn lock of dirt-gray hair and said, "Oh, Christian. Have you heard the woman who's been communing with the spirit of Beethoven? He's finished his Tenth Symphony and is using her as the instrument to bring it to this world from the other side. All the critics agree it is definitely done in his style and believe Ludwig has indeed made contact with her. Have you heard it?"

Mariette gasped as the fussy, nervous woman sputtered out her words. The lady looked as loony as her question. Mariette turned back to the man. Surely that question would raise his crooked eyebrow.

His expression didn't budge. "I'm sorry," he said. "I'm not familiar with that."

Mariette couldn't believe it. No one could endure all this inanity with such sobriety. The man's detachment was too unnatural. He had a three-ring circus going on around him, and he was blasé. *Good grief!* Was there no levity in the man? Or was he so accustomed to women showboating for him that it had no effect? His handsome face irked Mariette. There had to be a smile in the man somewhere.

Before she knew it, Mariette belted out, "Have you ever contacted a dead composer from the other side?"

Still, his face was solemn. With a low tired sigh, he said, "No, but I've cursed Liszt on occasion."

"Does he ever curse back?"

Suddenly, his aloofness broke. His eyebrows pinched together, and he looked around. Who was asking the questions? His eyes perused the crowd.

Mariette cocked her head to one side and gave him a cheeky grin.

A deep from-the-gut laugh overtook him. Finally, he was able to say, "Not yet."

The symphony's music director passed. Mariette watched as the crowd of women swarmed after the director. She turned back to the man. His eyes hadn't followed the women as they flocked away. They stayed riveted on her. He took a step toward her.

She took a step back. "Don't you get tired of answering such silly questions?"

"Yes."

"Then why do it?"

He perused the room. "Do you see the heavyset man over there in the gray business suit and the monocle?"

His gaze and toss of the head showed her where to look. In the crowd, she glimpsed a once probably athletic but now terribly rotund, jowly man with countless chins. The sheer size of the man caused her to gasp. "You mean Awful Otto? The one who looks like the villain from a 1940s cartoon?"

"Well, actually he's Cantankerous Klaus, but yes, that one. He's my manager. He likes me to make appearances at these sorts of things so I stay fresh in people's minds. And even though my next concert with this symphony is not for two years, he thinks I make good bait to toss out and pull back, thereby enticing them for the future."

"And what do you think?"

"After sixteen months touring in Europe, I think it's nice to be home."

"San Francisco?"

He nodded. "I was born here."

"Really?" She stared at his high cheekbones, wide-set eyes, and strong chin. Coupling that with the unusual pronunciation of some vowels, she said, "I would have thought you European. Probably Eastern European."

"My mother's Ukrainian. My father's Polish."

"What's that make you?"

"American."

"Touché."

"No, that's French. You have me at a slight disadvantage."

"How's that?"

"You know who I am, but I have absolutely no idea about you."

"I don't know who you are. I saw a crowd of women coming in here—so I joined them."

"A gate-crasher. Wonderful! Then I can dispose of the formality of finding someone acquainted with you who also knows me so they can give us a proper introduction." He held out his hand. "My name is Christian Stanislaus. How do you do?"

"Mariette Stuart. I'm doing just fine."

"Do you always crash such exciting things as volunteer recruitment?"

"Well, I'm in San Francisco for only two weeks. I want to see and do all kinds of things. This is the sort of cultural thing my mother would be glad I walked into. She bought the trip."

"Have you ridden the cable car to Fisherman's Wharf?"

"Not yet."

"Do you want to? With me? Now?"

"But we just met." She scrutinized him up and down. "You have any ID?"

His hand disappeared behind his left lapel and came up with a passport. He handed it to her.

Reading it, she said, "Hmm. You're six foot two. Twelve years older than me. Light brown hair, gray eyes. No wives or minors. You were born in California, and your signature is artistically illegible. Your photo is too stagey." She returned his passport. "I'd love to."

"Good. Is there any reason you couldn't leave through that door right now?" He pointed to a door marked "Exit" twelve feet away.

"Well, I have to go to coat check first to get my jacket."

"No. Don't. Just leave it. I'll see you get it later on. I promise. It's just that Klaus has been watching me talk with you. If you leave and return with your jacket, he's going to be all over me to make sure I stay put. If you just walk out those doors, you'll find yourself in a breezeway between the buildings. I'll meet you there in a minute."

Eyeing him suspiciously, she asked, "Do you do this often?"

"First time. That's why I'm so awkward at it."

She shot him a dubious glance and looked over his shoulder. "These doors here?"

He nodded. "Straight through these doors."

Mariette threw caution to the wind. She was on vacation. Why not go with this man? He was all dressed up. He even carried a passport. What could go wrong? It was still light outside. Besides, he didn't look dangerous.

In the breezeway, she'd just gotten her bearings when he ran up from behind. He grabbed her hand, and they fled like two kids ditching school. Running down Turk Street, she called out to him, "That was awfully fast. How'd you get past Otto?"

"Diversion. I had someone spill coffee on him."

Shaking her head, she laughed. "Awkward. Very awkward."

Christian pulled Mariette to a stop at the cable car turntable at Powell and Market Streets. "You wait here in line," he said. "I'll purchase us tickets."

Mariette got in line and watched Christian walk to the self-service machines. His long-legged stride was fluid and graceful. Smiling to herself, Mariette noted that he looked just as good at a distance from the rear as he did up close.

The corner of Market and Powell Streets was alive with people. Businessmen in three-piece suits with attaché cases sprinted off to luncheon meetings. Old Asian women with shopping bags slowly trundled up toward Chinatown. Adolescent boys skateboarded circles around giggling girls. Street-corner prophets vied for recognition and donations for their favored deities. Panhandlers made bids for spare change.

Mariette was still taking in the scene when Christian returned. "What's that funny noise I'm hearing?"

Christian said, "The clanging is the bell of the cable car coming down the hill. The whirring is the cable that's bringing it."

"And what about the trumpeting?"

"Trumpeting?"

"Like a bull elephant on the loose."

He quieted and listened again.

"That." She heard it again. "Right there. That."

"Oh. Foghorn."

"They're calling it in?" She laughed. "Why? Is it time to feed it?"

"No. It warns people it's coming."

"Hmm. Smart fog. Out of my way—here I come."

"No. It, the horn, warns that it, the fog, is coming."

"Oh." She gaped in mock horror. "You know, that shouldn't have made sense, but it does." She smiled. Verbal sparring with him was fun.

His smile reemerged, and he laughed.

She started to shiver. He took off his suit coat and wrapped it around her shoulders. The cable car arrived on the turntable, and they watched the conductors rotate the car. Jumping on, he told her to sit on the bench.

She protested, wanting to hang on to the side of the car like him.

"All right," he said. "But don't lean back, or you'll collide with a car going the other way."

"No."

"Yes."

The cable car started up the hill. The conductor clanged catchy rhythms on his bell and called out the names of the streets as he stopped at each corner. Ellis Street. O'Farrell Street. As they continued up Powell Street, Mariette hung on to the pole and leaned out to look back at where they had begun.

Christian grabbed hold of her and yanked forward just as a cable car sped by on the other track, missing her by inches.

Mouth open in shock, she turned to him.

He shook his head. "Tourist."

After one more block, the conductor called out, "Geary Boulevard."

When the cable car stopped, Christian pulled Mariette down.

She looked around. "I don't see any water. Where are the boats?"

"On the other side of the hill. This is Union Square."

He led her across the block-long park, past palm trees, benches, and people lounging on the grass. Walking into a department store on Post Street, he stopped the first salesgirl and asked where women's coats were.

"Sports or Better?" she said.

Christian turned to Mariette. "What kind of coat was it? You know the one you are now freezing without."

"Actually, this one is fine." She buried her nose in the collar of his suit coat and cuddled in, enjoying his masculine scent mixed with bay rum. "I'm quite warm."

"Yes, I know. But unfortunately, I'm not."

"Oh, all right." She turned to the salesgirl. "A camel-colored coat."

He bought her a camel hair coat, and they hopped the next cable car out to the wharf.

At Fisherman's Wharf, the piers teemed with fishing boats unloading their morning catches. Gigantic pots of boiling water were rooted to the ground and engulfed wriggling brown crabs and expelled them moments later stiff and livid red. Mounds of shaved ice filled heavy wooden boxes where shiny fish in all shapes and colors were nestled.

The smell of salt air, the sound of clanging boat tack and bellowing foghorns, and the sight of bustling fishermen, souvenir-laden street vendors, and camera-toting tourists caught Mariette all at once. She leaned against the wooden railing, letting her senses rouse and fill. It felt like she had slipped into a wonderland.

"Are you hungry?"

She looked up at Christian and held out her hand. "Yes."

He took it and gently pulled her to the nearest restaurant. "Do you like crab?"

She nodded as he pulled out a chair for her.

He ordered Crab Louie salads, sourdough french bread, and a bottle of Chardonnay.

Mariette hadn't realized her hunger until she found herself gulping french bread and butter as Christian tasted the wine and nodded acceptance to the sommelier. She stopped herself from gorging on a fourth slice and sat back. The two men discussed that year's grape harvest and the upcoming crush in California and Europe. Mariette wondered about this cosmopolitan gentleman with his manicured hands and polished ways. He was too good to be real. She took a sip of wine. It was excellent—just as she'd expected.

The salads arrived, and the sommelier left.

Christian filled both glasses, twisting the bottle with a flourish of the wrist to catch the final drop before it hit the smooth, starched white tablecloth. *He's showing off for me*, she thought.

Absentmindedly adjusting the Windsor knot in his blue shantung tie, he turned his attention to her. "How are you finding the wine?"

She looked down at her place and back up at him. "Right in front of me."

Chuckling, he leaned to one side and rested his forearm on the table. "That's where—not how."

"I find it delicious," Mariette replied. "Do you come here often?"

"No. First time. Can I ask you a personal question?" He moved his head to catch her glance.

She looked into the grayness of his eyes. "Shoot."

"Why are you only a sophomore? I'm unfamiliar with universities, having never gone, but I thought sophomores were nineteen or so."

"Usually, but I got married immediately out of high school. And when that didn't last, I decided I better take hold of my life and get on with it. I entered a women's reentry program."

"Women's reentry? Sounds aeronautical."

"No. It's just what they call having older women going back to school and feeling a part of it."

"Do you?" Christian asked.

She shook her head. "I'm still reeling from thinking I was all grown-up and should marry and settle down and move to the suburbs and have kids. Just like my mother did."

"What was wrong with what your mother did?"

"Nothing. But I married a man who did exactly what his father did. Keep wifey in the burbs, go to work in town, and sleep around." She shook her head. "It wasn't good enough. So, I divorced him."

Christian reached his hand across the table to touch hers. "I'm sorry. I didn't mean to pry."

The touch of his hand shocked her. "There was no sense in going on. He honestly believed what he did was the natural order of things. He'd never accept another way. Not deep inside where it counted." She shook her head. She couldn't believe she was telling this to a perfect stranger. Carlotta would have a fit. Before they went out for the evening, her best friend always said, "If we meet some men, don't talk about Robert. Men like to talk about themselves—not about your scummy ex-husband."

Feeling the gravity she'd weighed the air with, she pulled back from it and his hand. Shaking her head in mock reproof, she said, "You have the most annoying habit of listening."

He took her cue. Dropping the subject, he said, "You have the most appealing sense of humor."

"Some people find it peculiar."

"Some people have no taste."

"Why don't you let me listen for a while? Tell me what it's like to travel the world as a concert pianist?"

With a slight shrug, he said, "Pretty much as you'd imagine."

Mariette stared back. "I can't imagine anything."

"There's not much to tell. Playing onstage is heavenly, the culmination of all my dreams. The traveling is *schlect*. No good. At the end of the tour, I'm exhausted. I want nothing to do with the music. I just want to eat and sleep and recreate. Then, in three days, I'm dying to get back. I get like a fish out of water, gasping for my music to keep me alive."

She watched a spark start in his eyes as he talked. "You need the music that much?"

"I need the power of it. So, I make it mine." The spark started to blaze as he spoke. "In the way I play, what I play, it's all me. Total self-expression."

The busboy came and took the plates away.

Christian's intensity eased. "Right now, I'm a little expressed out. It was a long tour. That's why I was such a zombie at the auditorium earlier. In a few days, I'll be at my music again. I have to or I'll be miserable." He emptied his glass of wine. "I'll also be sued if I don't record the Rachmaninoff concerti I'm contracted to do this hiatus."

Abruptly, the alarm on his wristwatch sounded. Christian motioned the waiter over, paid the bill, escorted Mariette out the door into a taxi, and paid the cabbie to take her to the Fairmont Hotel. After helping her into the cab, Christian bowed, said, "Auf Wiedersehen," shut the door, and signaled for the cabbie to go.

Chapter 2

So abruptly did Mariette Stuart arrive back at her hotel room that she began to wonder if her interlude with the pianist wasn't just her imagination. Admittedly, she was lonely there with her best friend, Carlotta, coming down with appendicitis and backing out of the trip the last minute and her mother insisting she go before she got mired down in the suburbs for life, but even in her wildest dreams, she couldn't come up with a Christian Stanislaus. The smell of the aftershave from his jacket he wrapped around her still taunted with an occasional, elusive whiff.

Well, 'Ette. Face it. He's too smooth to be real, and too good-looking to be trusted. He's probably just another Robert in a fancier suit. But why did she spill her guts out to him at the restaurant with no more than his asking a simple question?

She plopped down on the bed. Feet still on the floor, she lay back, spread-eagle. Her mind wandered again. The feeling that had raced through her when he touched her hand at the restaurant was exciting and unnerving. So was the look in his eye when he talked about his music. She idly wondered what it would be like if he had that look in his eye for her. She shook her head and sat up. Consideration was useless. The terse ending of the day and his sudden retreat left little doubt their time together was over. Carlotta was right. No man wants to hear about some women's ex-husband.

Standing up, Mariette caught sight of herself in the mirror. Twirling around, she watched the lines of her coat flow. *A real camel hair coat!* The one she'd left behind was a factory outlet special. This one was from Saks. She smiled as she thought of how he felt the thickness and looked at the lining of two coats she'd tried on before he selected the better-made, probably more expensive of the two. The man certainly had nice taste in clothes. That suit coat he was wearing earlier was off no rack. Mariette wrapped her arms around herself and hugged the coat.

As she hung up the coat, three rapid knocks hit the door.

"Miss Stuart?"

She opened the door to a bellboy.

"Miss Mariette Stuart? A gentleman downstairs left this for you." He handed her two dozen long-stemmed pink roses around which was wrapped the jacket she'd left at the Civic Center Auditorium. The bellboy scratched his head. "That's the way it came."

Mariette took the roses and laughed. "That's fine. Is the gentleman still downstairs?"

"No. But there's a note there."

She tipped the bellboy and thanked him. She put the roses on the bed, unbuttoned the coat, lifted the stems, and rubbed her nose in the flowers. The feel was silky, the smell glorious. Grabbing the ice bucket from the bathroom, Mariette filled it with water and arranged the roses on the desk. She sat back on the bed and opened the note.

> Please have tea with the carp and me at the
> Japanese Tea Garden, Golden Gate Park.

Tomorrow. I'll be in the lobby coffee shop at
10:00 a.m. if you care to accept the invitation.
Regards,
Christian Stanislaus

Mariette read the card with its artistically illegible signature,
which after seeing once, she'd never miss. *Well, 'Ette. What do
you know about that, flowers and a retrieved coat? Now what?*
A part of her was intrigued. Another part of her recalled how
he said he needed three days of rest before getting back to his
music. The man was merely killing time between classes.

Chapter 3

Mariette Stuart fell deeply into a sleep busy with dreams of gray eyes darkening with excitement and cable cars that kept arriving back at her hotel room.

The next day, she woke up exhausted and spent at ten thirty. Jumping out of bed, she dared a cold shower. Instead of invigorating, it was nothing but cold. Even the towel was too soft to get her blood moving. All the rubbing did was slough off the water; it did not even absorb it. Maybe coffee would do the trick. As she finished applying makeup, Mariette remembered Christian's note about waiting in the downstairs coffee shop. Suddenly, there was a knock on the door.

"Just a second," she called. Mariette quickly pulled on a denim skirt and a madras blouse. Running her fingers through her short black hair, she figured there was no point in fussing with it; the fog would curl it anyway. She yanked the door open.

Christian's thoughtful expression broke into a warm smile when he saw her. "*Guten morgen* …er … good morning."

She stepped aside. "Please, come in."

She watched him stride to the middle of the room. Dark gray slacks clothed his long legs. An ice blue cashmere turtleneck topped with a gray herringbone sport coat covered his muscular chest. With his light brown hair tossed loosely back and his gray eyes picking up a light blue tint from the sweater, he looked so perfect it struck Mariette the man probably looked elegant in his underwear.

He stopped and turned.

"You left abruptly yesterday," Mariette said.

"Yes, I did. Did you get your coat?"

"Oh, yes. Of course." She went to the coatrack, picked up the camel hair coat, and gave it to him.

He walked around behind her and placed the coat over her shoulders. "It may be a tad warm for this at the park right now, but you'll need it later on."

She shrugged the coat off. "Oh, no!" She turned toward him. "I thought you wanted it back."

His brow furrowed as he caught the coat before it fell. "I bought the coat because I inconvenienced you by having you abandon the one you came in. I retrieved that one because I promised you I would. I always keep my promises. That's why I left so abruptly. I had to get back to the auditorium before they locked up. Both coats are yours."

"Look, Christian. I know yesterday was just a handy diversion for us both."

His hand shot out to stop her and the sick feeling in his gut. "Oh, my dear. That was in no way what I had in mind. I'm sorry if you got that impression. I know I can be very impulsive, but there is thought behind the impulse. I saw a woman who is attractive and witty and whom I wanted to know before she slipped from my life. I apologize if my suddenness seemed rash and made you feel used as a *diversion*."

"Christian, you are a very sweet man, and I thank you for the coat and for showing me the wharf, but I really don't think we should continue this."

"Why not?"

They watched each other.

He nudged her with his elbow and flashed his smile. "Come on. The carp are waiting. You can tell me on the way."

"Playing tour guide again, eh?" Mariette shook her head. How could any man be so endearing and overwhelming at the same time? Oh, well. She was on vacation. Inappropriate infatuations were what vacations were all about.

Chapter 4

The Japanese Tea Garden in Golden Gate Park was beautiful. Purple-red leafed trees lined tiny walks that curved through the garden. The walks turned into ramps and bridges that spanned ponds. Inside the ponds, the carp were bright orange and shiny black, big as trout. Mariette held on to the bamboo rail and leaned forward to inspect the biggest goldfish she'd ever seen. The carp passed in slow motion, occasionally coming to the surface to snap at a floating bug. It was pleasant to watch the parade of their tranquil lives.

Christian handed Mariette a penny. "Make a wish and toss."

She looked back in the pond. So that's what the shiny circles in the bottom were. "Is it good luck?"

"Could be."

She closed her eyes, flipped the penny, and watched it sink down to the bottom. "Aren't you throwing one?"

"I already have."

"Does it work?"

Watching the green-eyed sprite with her dimples and curly black hair standing before him, he smiled. "I think so."

Christian took Mariette's hand and led her up the path to the pavilion. As they passed the ancient Japanese Buddha, she wondered how everything could be so serene while she was getting butterflies at just having her hand held.

They sat at a table on wooden stools, and Christian ordered green tea. It came with salty little square crackers and fortune cookies. The crackers were wonderful: rice and soy and crunch. The fortune cookies she eschewed, and he followed suit.

"What sort of courses are you taking at university?" Christian asked.

"Well, I'm still a lower-level undergraduate. I'm fulfilling a lot of requirements now."

"Requirements for what degree?"

"Oh, a bachelor of science degree."

"In?"

"Some sort of biological science. My counselor keeps pushing medicine, nursing."

"And you're not interested in being Florence Nightingale?"

"No, I hate hospitals. They're full of sick people. I want to be where life is vibrant. Moving. I want to be in the water. Oceans and lakes and rivers and all kinds of marine life."

Christian smiled at the chord he'd finally struck. "Then, why don't you?"

"My counselor says it's not practical. It's a million-to-one chance I'd ever be an oceanographer."

"Why? Are the oceans drying up?"

"No, just my chances. What with being late getting started."

"Million to one, huh?" Christian reached for her hand, but she put it down on her lap and he didn't pursue it. "If I listened to everyone who told me there wasn't a chance in hell I'd be a virtuoso pianist, I'd still be tuning pianos with my father on Clement Street."

"You were a piano tuner?"

He nodded. "Apprentice."

"And it didn't work out?"

"Oh, it would have worked out." He refilled their cups with tea. "I mean physically I'm capable of it. I have the dexterity and the ear. But spiritually, it didn't. I couldn't get that close to the instrument what with weighting the action, setting the strike of the hammers, tuning the strings, and turning it over for someone else to hear its sound and enjoy its voice while I just walked away. That ate at my soul every time. I've got to be the one to make the sound and hear its voice. My life depends on it."

He looked down and back up at her. "Believe in yourself. Then take the risks to get what you want in life." He picked up the plate and offered her one of the fortune cookies.

Eyeing the cookies, she debated and chose. She cracked it open and read aloud: "'Trust him but keep your eyes open.'"

He cracked the other cookie and read the fortune aloud. "'Live by your wits, not your artistry.' Hmm, another dissenter."

The path leaving the pavilion winded to a high-arched moon bridge. The bridge was vertical on either side with a short stilted arch connecting its two piers. It could be scaled by using the narrow wooden slats nailed into the vertical piers as toeholds while grasping the handrail for support. They began climbing together, but Christian was over and down the other side before Mariette saw how he did it. The climbing up Mariette figured easily, but at the top, she stopped when she looked down to the ground.

On the ground, Christian looked up at her. "Turn around and back down."

"So you can look up my skirt?"

He turned away. "I will demurely avert my eyes."

"Yeah, and pigs fly."

"Do they do that in Ohio too?" Christian held his hand up to Mariette. "Come on. You can make it."

"I don't think so."

He leaned up as far as he could, and his face was a yard away from her. "Risk it. I dare you." He turned and walked away.

She watched him walk out of sight. Turning around, she held fast to the handrail. Her leg stretched down until it touched a wooden slat. She tried the other leg. Both feet held on the same slat. The next step was easier. She reached the bottom. She was on solid ground. Immediately, she ran around to the other side of the moon bridge and climbed back up and down again. When she finished, Christian sauntered up.

Mariette turned on him. "How long would you have left me stranded up there?"

"Until the fire department arrived."

Mariette punched Christian's bicep.

He held her fist to stop the second blow. "I knew you'd do it. You flew two thousand miles to vacation by yourself in a strange city. You divorce your husband because his cheating on you wasn't 'good enough.' You start school after that divorce to take 'hold of your life.' You've got guts. I believed you'd do it." He let go of her fist. "Believe in yourself. I do."

When they walked out of the Japanese Tea Garden, Christian asked, "Where did you learn to jab like that? My arm still hurts."

"My dad was a boxer in the navy. He taught my mother and me to defend ourselves."

Rubbing his bicep, Christian said, "Well, use it with kindness. It's a damn near lethal weapon."

Mariette was exhausted and exuberant. She watched Christian as they walked along. She didn't know what to make of him. Was he savior, teacher, or bully?

When they reached John F. Kennedy Drive in Golden Gate Park, Christian turned to Mariette. "Would you like me to take you back to your hotel?"

"Actually, yes." She breathed a sigh of relief. It was if he'd read her mind. "I'm more tired than I would have expected."

***

Riding the elevator to her room, Christian said,

"Would you favor me with your company at breakfast tomorrow? There's a wonderful little restaurant in Sutro Heights overlooking the ocean. You can see Seal Rock, Ocean Beach, and the Pacific. The food is all-American diner fare, but the waitress is delightful—and the view makes your knees weak. I'd love for you to see it."

The eagerness in his face tugged at her heart. *He wants to show me something he feels is special. Oh, well, one more day can't possibly hurt.* "Still playing the tour guide, eh? All right. How's nine o'clock?"

"Perfect."

Coming to her hotel room door, Mariette turned her back to the door and faced Christian.

He bowed to her. *"Auf Wiedersehen."* His eyes searched her face from the high forehead with its widow's peak to the deep green eyes, from the high cheekbones to the pink Cupid's bow mouth. Smiling, he said, "Incidentally, that means 'until I see you again' not 'good-bye forever.'" He jammed his hands into his pockets and walked away, calling over his shoulder. "Tomorrow at nine."

Walking down the hallway, Christian hoped against hope that he hadn't come on too strongly and frightened her. He was all too aware that his method of achievement while successful on the stage could be overwhelming in person.

25

Once inside the room, Mariette leaned back against the door and slid down its length to the floor. One minute she wanted Christian close enough to feel his breath on her, and the next second, she wanted to push him away and run.

Mariette picked up the bedside phone. All of a sudden, she was starving. She ordered a burger and fries from room service. Nice comforting back-home food. When it arrived, she wolfed it down and stared at the crumbly remains on her plate. What had he said? "'Believe in yourself. Then take the risks to get what you want in life.'" Impossible. She slammed the cover down on the plate.

Turning on the television, she let her mind go on hold until she drifted off to sleep.

Chapter 5

The next morning, Mariette woke up in plenty of time to be dressed and ready for Christian's arrival. In the shower, she adjusted the water extra hot for a good old-fashioned purge. "Wash away the previous day to start with one that's new." That was what her father had taught. At home, she could always tell the purging was done when the water ran cold. At her hotel, the hot water appeared to be endless. She gave up outwaiting it before she started to wrinkle like a prune.

Mariette pulled on a pair of blue jeans, rolling the pant legs halfway up her calves to create fat cuffs. A blue-and-white striped short-sleeved top with a scoop neck coupled with brown sandals completed the outfit. She went to the mirror and looked. Giving herself two thumbs-up, she said, "Okay! For an Ohio beach, anyway."

Promptly at nine o'clock, there was a knock on the door. Going to answer it, Mariette idly hoped he'd be dressed in an acid-green polyester leisure suit. She braced herself and opened it. Their eyes met and locked. Then, she laughed.

"Okay!" she said with satisfaction.

Christian allowed himself the rudeness of staring. The blue denim of her jeans tightly encased her hips, flowed past slender thighs, and curled up to reveal tight, muscular calves and neatly turned ankles. Her unrestrained bosom stretched tightly one pale blue stripe of a top that barely covered her midriff and revealed a slender waist. She looked so adorable! A sailor cap was all she needed.

"Okay, what?" he asked. "I'm on time? I'm whom you were expecting? What?"

"You're finally dressed normally."

He laughed, making a mental note and saying, "The lady's sartorial preference is blue jeans and a T-shirt. Check."

"Tight T-shirt," she said. "It shows off your chest muscles."

"I believe that's my line."

"Beat you to it."

"Hungry?"

"Starved. Ever since I arrived."

He held up his hand and turned away. "That line I won't bandy with." He escorted her out the door.

They were greeted at the restaurant by an elderly woman with flowers braided through the plaits in her hair. Bearing armfuls of filled dishes, she paused long enough for a greeting. "Ah, *Klavierspieler* with lady. How nice to see. There is a free table over there." She motioned with her head. "Or if you wish to wait, a booth by the window will open soon."

Christian nodded. "The lady is from out of town and favors the ocean. We'll wait."

Mariette watched the woman in the dirndl bustle away. The waitress deposited the eggs and pancakes and waffles at a window-side table, chatting briefly with the customers and smiling all the while.

Mariette looked up at Christian, "What did she call you?"

Christian said, "*Klavierspieler*. It's German. Literally, it translates as piano player."

"Piano player?" Mariette laughed. "That's great. Not nearly as stuffy as 'virtuoso pianist.'"

"Are you inferring I'm stuffy? I take umbrage with that, my dear woman."

"Come on. The booth's free." Mariette led Christian to the table and checked out both sides to see which afforded the better view. Mariette settled in the booth facing south; the ocean and the Sutro Bath ruins were on her right. "I'll sit over here. You've already seen the Pacific Ocean. Probably from both sides."

He nodded. "Smack dab in the middle too."

"Show-off."

Christian slid into the seat opposite and watched her face as Mariette stared out the window. He couldn't believe his good fortune. This spunky young girl with black curls around her face wandered into his life as irresistible as a puppy. Oh, how he wanted to scoop her up and secret her away before someone else lured her in.

Mariette looked out the window. The ocean was glassy blue. The waves were huge. Building the water higher and higher, the wave curled in on itself and spilled out onto the beach. The blue glass turned to white foam, coating everything in its path and disappearing into the sand. Watching that wave until it was mere bubbles in the beach, Mariette looked back toward the horizon. Another wave rushed to take its place. She was beguiled, but she had expected no less.

The waitress arrived with a thermos full of coffee, immediately turned over the cups, and poured as she spoke. "And will you both have coffee, my dears? The sausage is made fresh this morning and is very good. The fresh fruit bowl is apples, melons, strawberries, and late-summer peaches. Would you like some more time or do you know now?" She turned to Christian. "The usual?" He nodded.

She turned to Mariette. "And you, my dear?"

Realizing the abrupt silence was requiring her attention, Mariette turned from the ocean's mesmerizing draw. "I'm sorry. What was it?"

"Anna wants to know what you're having for breakfast."

"Oh." Mariette looked blankly at the menu. "This is terrible, but I think I want blueberry pancakes."

"It's not terrible," the waitress said. "The pancakes are quite good." She took both menus. "It's nice to have someone at the table enjoying more than dry wheat toast and poached eggs."

"Who's having that?" Mariette asked.

Anna angled her head toward Christian, muttering as she walked away. "Der Klavierspieler."

Mariette chuckled. "Piano player. I love that." She perused Christian's face. Going to bed with the notion, she woke with it still unresolved. How does one turn fantasy into reality? "So, how does the piano tuner from Clement Street wind up being piano player to the world?"

"Good looks and timing."

Glibness, she didn't need. "Seriously. And don't tell me practice."

His next line anticipated, Christian's gaze went to his coffee cup. How to put it all together? It was such a long time ago. Another lifetime. Owing her an answer, he tried to put himself back in that place. The atmosphere of the house. The smell of sauerbraten from the kitchen mingling with pipe tobacco from the music rooms. The sound of constant music— some excellent, some wanting. And the awe the man evoked.

Slowly, Christian warmed to the scenario as he spoke. "My father used to take me out with him to various clients. At first, it was just to hand him tools and stay out of the way. Finally, it was to pay attention and learn. One day, we went to the home of a master piano teacher. A maestro. Straight line of descent from Beethoven. Teacher to pupil. Teacher to pupil. As I helped my father tighten strings on one piano, I could hear Maestro giving lessons on another. I was overwhelmed. I wanted to be there. Something told me I was supposed to be there. When we were through, I asked my father if I could take lessons from the man. My father said he'd given me enough piano lessons for what I needed to know in life."

"And you didn't accept that?"

"No. I waited about a week, and then I went to Maestro's house and told him I was there to tighten any tuning that had slipped. That it was part of the service."

"After only a week?"

"As soon as you start playing a piano, it starts going out of tune. Since he had droves of students banging away on these two instruments, it wasn't too untoward a thing for a twelve-year-old to come up with."

"Twelve-year-old?" Mariette snorted. "Prodigy."

"Well, to make a long story interminable, as I tuned one piano, I'd listen to the lesson Maestro was giving on the other. Then I'd copy it. So, while tuning two pianos, I'd hear two, maybe three lessons. One day, I was playing the lesson Maestro had just taught when he came in. He instructed me that my staccato would improve if I lifted my wrist while I played. He demonstrated what he meant.

"After I grasped the technique to his satisfaction, he asked if my father knew I was there. I couldn't lie to him, and I said no. Being there had been my own idea. So, he calls my father, tells him what I've been doing, and says he wants to take me on as a pupil."

"You adopted him—and he wanted you?"

"Yes. Apparently, he heard something he couldn't walk away from. As he told me years later, a teacher is only as good as his pupil. He wanted us both to be the best."

31

"What did your father say?"

"He didn't know whether to glow with pride for the honor of Maestro wanting to teach his son or knock my block off for being such a wisenheimer. But seeing as he left his homeland and traveled six thousand miles to capture his dream, I guess he figured it was futile to stand in the way of mine." Christian held up his hand. "We are very much alike."

"Driven?"

"Stubborn as hell. When I'm with him, he still doesn't know whether to glow with pride or knock my block off."

Anna came to take away plates and refill the coffee cups. She turned to Mariette and said, "Is his charm grabbing you?"

"I try to resist."

"Don't try too hard."

Mariette laughed.

Turning back to Christian, Mariette found him deep in thought. A poignant, sad look was on his face.

"Did I have you bring up something painful?"

Gradually, Christian pulled from his thoughts. "The only thing painful about it was the leaving. It was a wonderful studious time. Days on end of playing music, discussing interpretations, feeding off Maestro's thoughts, adding my own. It was very heady and satisfying. Before all the 'theatrics' as my father would say." With a wave of his hand, he indicated his garb. Then realizing he wasn't dressed in his wing-collar shirt, bow tie, and tailcoat, he dropped his hand to his lap and chuckled at himself.

"Then why did you leave?"

"Because it was time. One can't stay in the same place or one stagnates. That wasn't what Maestro was teaching me. I'd already 'seen.' Now, it was time to 'do' on a large scale. Which is where Maestro's nephew, my manager—"

"Cantankerous Klaus?"

Christian nodded and finished the sentence, "Comes in."

Mariette refilled their coffee cups from the thermos. "Let me see if I have this straight. Your father's client becomes your teacher. Your teacher's nephew becomes your manager."

"Right."

Shaking her head, Mariette dismissed its usefulness. "Sounds like an awful lot of nepotism to me."

"Of course it is. What's wrong with that? Human beings are a familial species. It's how we survive." Christian took a sip of coffee, realizing it was starting to make him shake—or maybe that was her effect on him. "You miss one important point though. No one would ever have come up to me and asked if I wanted to be 'piano player to the world.' I had to instigate that on my own."

Her eyes turned serious and remote. She was gnawing something over in her head. Finally, she said, "Does it bother you that you disappointed him?"

"Who?"

"Your father."

"My *father*? I don't believe I have. I've surprised him, yes. He always expected his middle son to be … unadventurous. Stick close to home. Stay in his business. But I have too much respect for him to believe he'd be thwarted just because one of his preconceived expectations wasn't met. He's more magnanimous than that.

"And what of your father?"

She turned and looked out the window. On a huge rock rising from the ocean, a lone fisherman cast his rod while balancing himself. He was a good thirty feet up from the water. She wondered how he got up the side of such a steep rock. Gazing around, she noticed a narrow causeway maybe twelve inches wide running from the rock to the shore. She shook her head. How'd the fisherman manage that long, thin strip laden with rod, bucket, and bait without falling?

Mariette turned back to Christian. "My father was an old-fashioned man. Firmly believed in the Protestant work ethic."

"He's no longer living?"

She finished her coffee and cradled the cup in both hands. "He died at work. He was a bank president. One day, he got impatient waiting for a custodian to change a pulsing fluorescent bulb, so he climbed on his desk to do it himself. He reached up, and his heart ripped in two. They said his lips were turning blue before they could lay him on the floor."

"I'm sorry."

"I'm not." The coffee cup was placed back on the table. "If his heart hadn't failed him, my divorce would have broken it."

His brow furrowed. "Why do you say that?"

She turned back to the window. "Because he said the day I was married was the happiest day of his life. My divorcing would undo all that."

He leaned forward to catch her attention away from the window. "Were you happy the day you got married?"

Her gaze out the window wouldn't budge. "Of course."

"Maybe his happiness was not for the marriage itself but for seeing you happy. Are you an only child?"

Mariette turned on him. With eyes void of feeling, she nodded. "Daddy's little girl. His 'one in a million.'"

The bitterness in her voice made him cringe. "If you were that precious to him, I doubt he'd want your memory of him crippled with such guilt. It's unfair all around for you to decide what his reaction would have been."

Mariette turned away. "What do you know?"

"Of this situation, nothing at all." The alarm on Christian's wristwatch sounded. He quickly turned it off. "Would you please excuse me? Being incommunicado for three days, the 'wayward talent' should really check in with his manager. Klaus spends Wednesday mornings with his mistress. He's in a good mood afterward. Positively buoyant."

The look on Christian's face was of the recalcitrant child with his hand caught in the cookie jar. Mariette laughed. "Tell me, if Klaus is so cantankerous, why do you have him as your manager?"

"Because 98 percent of the time, he is absolutely brilliant."

"And the other 2 percent?"

"The *talent* becomes wayward."

"You're the *talent*?"

"His pet name for me. He's the brains; I'm the talent."

In mimicry of Christian, Mariette cocked an eyebrow. "I find the *simplism* of that doubtful."

Laughing, Christian stood. "I won't be long."

She watched him go to the pay phone by the door. She studied him as he placed his call. He took himself so seriously and so lightly at the same time. She found it confusing and fascinating. And she envied the way he spoke of the people in his life with such understanding and acceptance.

Chapter 6

Seeing the fisherman leaving the rock, Mariette realized that was where she wanted to be. Passing Christian by the door, she put her hand on the small of his back. "I'm going down to the beach."

Christian nodded.

Mariette leaned in close, asking *sotto voce*, "Where are you saying we're calling from?"

"Reno."

Knowing people went to Reno, Nevada, not only to gamble but also for quickie marriages, Mariette whooped. "You really are wayward."

Mariette strolled down the sidewalk, past the restaurant, and over to the sand. Finding the causeway that led up and out from the beach, she walked heel to toe until she claimed the rock the fisherman just deserted. She sat and faced the ocean. To her left, Seal Rock was occupied by dozens of sleek inhabitants that barked at one another, slipped into the ocean, and waddled back into place.

Farther out toward the horizon, a flock of birds flew in a V formation. Allowing for distance, the birds looked quite large and almost prehistoric. As the huge birds flew, the leader periodically dipped down and back up. Each bird in line followed suit when it arrived at that precise point. The line undulated as it flew. *Of course,* she thought. *Pelicans!* She'd only seen them in museums and on television. It thrilled her to watch them.

A seagull flew overhead. She turned to watch it. As it got closer to the shore, it was suddenly lifted up, wings outstretched and motionless. She waited to see how long it could hold the pose. Standing up, she spread her arms, wishing she could grab the updraft and float up. Oh, how she wanted to be part of this ocean. To make it hers. She remembered how descriptions and pictures of it made her feel as a child. Pacific. It made her feel that way now, peaceful and fulfilled. Pacific.

Was he right about her and risks? Was she too scared to dare? She liked to think not, but what was the reality? She watched the seagull holding itself so high in the thermals. She was going to do it. She wanted to study oceans and marine life. She could do it. She could fly that high.

As the seagull furled its wings and dove into the ocean, a wave washed the rock, sweeping Mariette from it.

Chapter 7

"So where are you?" Klaus Steiner asked Christian Stanislaus.

"Reno."

"Oh, please. Have some pity for an old man's heart."

Christian snorted. The "old man" was a mere ten years his senior. "I'm in the city."

"What are you up to?"

"Stretching my fingers for the Rachmaninoff."

"So, you haven't forgotten the recording session?"

"Do I ever forget anything?"

"You don't forget—you ignore. You could have told me you wanted to leave the auditorium the other day."

"And what would you have said?"

"Find a more propitious time."

"That's why I didn't tell you."

"*Krystia.*"

Christian groaned as his manager started using his informal family nickname.

Klaus continued his soothing tones. "I understand a young man has his urges that need quenching. *Bitte!* Be careful. Watch out for yourself. The thought of you getting involved with a woman again makes my ulcer kick."

As Christian listened, he wondered who benefited most from their willful child versus overprotective mother hen scenes.

"Do you hear me?"

Probably, they both did. It was a way to acknowledge their pervading interdependency.

"*Krystia?*"

"I'm listening."

"You listen, but do you hear?"

Through a picture window, Christian saw Mariette on the rock. He gasped in disbelief. What in the world was she doing on a boulder in the ocean with an incoming tide?

"Yes, Klaus. I hear you, and I will be at the recording studio first thing tomorrow morning. I promise. *Auf Wiedersehen.*"

As Christian raced down the beach, waves boomed against the rock where Mariette no longer stood. Throwing off his jacket, he ran into the water. Only one thought surfaced in his mind: he had to fight the undertow. Every year, it claimed people foolish enough to challenge it. He had to get them both to survive it.

His adrenaline racing, he swam to where she'd gone in. He dove down, scrambling around furiously while the air in his lungs held. There was no sign of her. Bouncing up, he gasped for air. Lungs filled, he plummeted again. He let himself be pulled with the outgoing tide until his air could no longer sustain him.

Springing up quickly, he gasped air and plunged again. As he dove down, an elbow knocked his chin. Grabbing at the arm, he pulled up toward the surface. When they both reached the air, he shook her fiercely. "Don't fight me or you'll drown us both." He placed her hands on his shoulders, eased her onto his back, and started for shore.

He was a good swimmer but not a particularly strong one. Concentrating one stroke at a time, he focused on the jacket he'd thrown down on the beach. Feeling the current's pull that would tire and ultimately exhaust him, Christian tried to recall the first time he lapped Larson Pool. The swimming instructor's directions of envisioning one perfect stroke and repeating it over and over had dwarfed the pool, and the ten-year-old had felt he could swim to Alcatraz and back. Christian replayed that memory in his mind as he swam. Finally, they arrived on shore.

Gently prying her fingers from around his throat, he let her drop. His heart pounded fiercely, and his breath rasped. He glared at the little girl crumpled in the sand. His blood coursed violently through his veins. He wanted her so badly that it hurt. He wanted to feel himself deep inside her throbbing and pulsating and filling her until she screamed his name in anguish and desire.

He closed his eyes and turned away. What kind of a sick bastard pulls a girl from the water and attacks her? Where was all his self-possession? Or was that on hiatus too? He lay down on the beach, respiring deeply until his heart and breath slowed. Finally, he said, "You know risks don't have to be life-threatening. In fact, it's better if they're not."

Still hunched in the sand, shaken and wet, Mariette looked at Christian. She wanted to hit him, scream at him, to wrap his arms around her, and cry on his chest. Then she saw the posted sign.

Danger
Hazardous Conditions
Cliff and Surf Areas Extremely Dangerous
People Have Been Swept from Rocks and Drowned

Drownings Occur Annually
Due to Surf and Severe Undertow
Please Remain Safely on Shore

Her heart sank. She hadn't noticed it before. She wasn't taking any risks. She was just being oblivious and foolhardy. And she could have drowned them both.

Picking herself up, Mariette started brushing sand from her legs and arms. And she was the one who wanted to be the oceanographer? She hadn't even bothered to watch the tide or read the sign.

Christian picked up his sweatshirt jacket and brought it over to Mariette. "I think we should go to hospital. Make sure you haven't swallowed too much salt water."

She shrugged off the jacket and turned on him. "I haven't swallowed any salt water. I know how to swim. In fact, I have lifeguard credentials."

He backed away from her ire, both hands up to show he was not pursuing it further.

She watched him retreat in his posture of nonaggression. Good heavens, what was she doing? He'd just saved her life. When he grabbed her, she had been swimming all out against the undertow. And losing. If it weren't for him, she'd just be another drowning statistic. She held out her hand to him. "I'm sorry."

He nodded and—with a wave of his hand—indicated her apology wasn't necessary.

They stood in a standoff. Each was unsure about what to do or say next. Finally, Mariette said, "I'm leaving tomorrow, you know?"

"I know."

"Right now, I'd like to go back to my hotel room and take a nice hot bath. Then, tonight, I want to invite you out to dinner in appreciation of … everything."

Fighting his urges, Christian squared his shoulders and pulled himself to his full height. "I'd be honored."

"I'll make a reservation for six. We can walk from my hotel room at five thirty." She saw a cab turn in toward the Cliff House taxi stand and waved it down. Picking up his jacket from the sand, she handed it to him. "Until tonight."

He watched Mariette Stuart run toward the cab.

Before getting in, she called his name.

Looking away from the ocean, he saw not the girl he met three days ago but a glimpse of the woman she was to be.

"Thank you."

The finesse and sincerity in her voice shook him to his core. He watched the cab drive away and walked back to the little restaurant.

When he walked in the door, Anna gave him a bewildered look and a sad smile. "Lose her already?"

"We're meeting again for dinner. Right now, I'd like an Anchor Steam, *bitte*.

From the booth, he glared at the rock and the waves booming against it. If he'd lost her now that he'd found her, he'd be devastated.

Anna brought the beer and poured it for him. Pointing to the water and his soaked state, she asked, "You go in on such a cold, foggy day?"

Christian nodded. "*Ja*, Anna. I went in. Right over my head."

Chapter 8

Mariette snuggled into her warm herbal bath of lavender leaves and juniper twigs at her suite at the Fairmont Hotel in San Francisco. She played with the water, slapping it over her shoulders, lying back into it, blowing bubbles, and rising like a seal, hair plastered to her skull.

She tried to block the recurrence, but its insistence was not to be denied. Over and over, it played out in her mind. One minute she was secure on the rock, and the next, she was in the water. The thought that she had to surface was what she remembered most. Surfacing was paramount, but she'd lost all sense of which way was up. It was terrifying. When Christian grabbed her, she thought something was pulling her down. Flailing and stroking all at once, she'd hit him several times before she became aware of his intent.

Getting her back to shore in the manner that he had was definitely not a Red Cross–sanctioned method, but it worked. She imagined all things went that way for him: unorthodox but successful. She thought of the breadth and hardness of the shoulder muscles that had swum her in. He really was a very strong man. She submerged, once again blowing bubbles.

Yes, she wanted the water and the ocean, but did it want her? Her head leaned back against the tub's ledge, and she saw the seagull riding so high in the thermals. Some of that was what she needed. That feeling of being part of and flowing with the world around her—not being knocked around and overtaken by it.

So what was the trick? How could one break from the way life was pushing her without getting herself broken in the process? She'd tried going through the proper channels of school and counselors, and she'd been stopped cold. A branch of lavender floated by; she instantly seized it. How could she become one in a million and get off Clement Street?

Mariette sighed. She hadn't had a father who was a marine biologist, and she didn't know anyone who knew Jacques Cousteau or anyone else in that field. Besides, nepotism was bad news. Firsthand experience had taught her that relatives and business didn't mix, especially when the bank president brings home the hotshot young protégé from his office who winds up marrying the boss's eighteen-year-old daughter. She submerged herself back in the water and blew more bubbles to get Robert out of her brain.

There had to be another way to succeed. What would Christian have done if they'd banished him from the building where he was sneaking lessons? Would he have given up and accepted defeat? Probably not. Mariette pulled the plug from her tub. It didn't seem like much stopped him.

She looked over at the Chinese red silk evening dress with black dragons woven through the brocade. Going through Chinatown earlier, her cab got stuck in traffic. Impatient and wet, Mariette decided it was faster on foot. Letting the taxi go, she found herself face-to-face with a clothing store. In the window was the most exotic dress she'd ever seen. As she dried herself, she thought, *Let's see him outdress this one.*

Promptly at five thirty, there was a knock on the door. Mariette stepped into her heels and smoothed down the tight skirt. Smiling, she opened the door and waved him in.

"You didn't mention how far we are from the restaurant, but …" Christian strode into the room and stopped in his tracks, mouth open.

She smiled at his speechlessness. "Oh, it's just up Telegraph Hill. Ten, fifteen minutes away." She took the white chrysanthemums from his hands and plucked one flower from its stem. "Oh, perfect." Leaning toward the mirror, she pinned it in her hair. "Thank you."

Mouth still agape, slowly nodding, Christian's gaze traveled the length of Mariette's form-fitting dress. The Mandarin collar fanned out to a tight, sleeveless bodice and darted in to pinch her tiny waist. The cloth flared out to stretch snugly over her hips with the skirt slit halfway up her right thigh. He loved every black dragon woven into the shiny red brocade of the cloth.

Grinning with satisfaction, she motioned to his black business suit. "I know I'm leaving tomorrow, but you didn't have to dress so funereal. Don't you have any evening clothes?"

Feeling like a schoolboy caught with his head in the clouds, he stammered, "Uh, dinner jacket?"

She shook her head. "White tie and tails."

"Oh, evening coat. Sure." He pulled himself up straight, trying to collect himself. "Yes, of course. I didn't realize the occasion was formal."

"It's not," she teased and headed for the door.

Following her out, he shook his head. Maybe it wasn't formal, but it was definitely getting serious.

The restaurant on Telegraph Hill was a castle that overlooked San Francisco Bay. Dark mahogany paneling covered the walls. Deep burgundy carpeting blanketed the floors. The tables were dressed in starched white linen with a single yellow rose in a crystal bud vase. Their table looked out on the San Francisco–Oakland Bay Bridge; the long fingers of five different piers were beneath with Alcatraz Island dead ahead and Angel Island beyond that.

Mariette ordered oysters in puff pastry with leek sauce and perused the wine list. Looking through the book of wine labels, she started getting confused under the waiter's gaze. She knew white wine went with shellfish. She turned to Christian. "Are you having seafood too?"

"I'll pass on ocean inhabitants for a while." He turned to the waiter. "Prime rib. Rare, please."

Mariette flipped back and forth through the pages. What went with oysters and beef?

The waiter placed his hand on one of the pages and tapped his little finger.

"How about a Louis Martini zinfandel?" Mariette said.

The waiter smiled and retrieved the book. "Excellent choice, madam."

Christian sat back in his chair, impressed. "Yes, it is."

Mariette leaned forward, resting her hand by the bud vase. "So, you think I should go in for oceanography?"

Christian rested his hand on the other side of hers. "Mariette, it doesn't matter what I think. It matters what you want. It's your life. Live it for yourself. Not to please others."

"Yes, I know. But—"

"There is no *but*. That's all there is. Believe in yourself and take the risks to get what you want in life."

"And hope no one drowns in the process." Her words slipped out before she knew it, which shocked them both.

Finally, he uncurled his fingers and reached out to touch her hand. "Temper it with a little fear," he said gently. "It keeps you from being reckless. Reckless people don't live long."

His touch on her hand sent sparks through her.

"You make it sound simple," Mariette said. "Believing and risking. Knowing which risks to take and which to fear."

"I don't mean it to. It isn't simple, but it is addictive," Christian said. "You get to where you won't abide living any other way."

The waiter brought the wine. Mariette tasted, nodded, and raised her glass to Christian. "What do you think?"

He raised his glass to hers and tasted. "Very nice."

Feeling proficient, Mariette swirled the wine in her glass and held it up to watch it flow back down to the bowl. "Great legs." She took another sip. "Good nose and full body."

Christian squirmed nervously. Somehow, he wasn't very hungry.

"Do you have any fears?"

"Of course."

She smiled at him coyly and tossed her head to one side. "For instance."

Watching her eyes, Christian slowly moved his fingers across her knuckles. "Terribly weighty ones." He encircled her first knuckle with his index finger. "Fear of missing my flight." He stroked down her fingers. "Fear of winding up in the wrong concert hall." Sliding his hand over hers, he rested this thumb beneath her palm. "Fear of losing my place in the middle of a piece while playing on stage." His thumb pushed gently into her cupped hand.

That maneuver was beginning to make her sweat. "Oh, no. Catastrophe. What do you do then?"

Caressing her knuckles with the pads of his fingers, he kept his thumb resting against her palm. "Break into a cold sweat and fake it."

She swallowed. "I bet you're good at that."

"The former or the latter?"

She could feel the blood pounding in her ears. "Both."

"Be careful, now!" Setting down two plates, the waiter warned. "That plate was in the oven. They're hot now. Don't touch." He hurried away. "*Bon appétit.*"

Her hand released, Mariette instinctively adjusted her plate. "Ow." She put the burnt finger to her mouth. She looked at Christian. His gaze had never left her.

"Why isn't a man like you married?"

Christian sat back in his chair. He wasn't sure what she thought a man like him was, but her question was legitimate. "Because, until now, I never found anyone who interested me."

"Never?"

"Not really."

"Then, what really?"

He shrugged. "I was engaged once, but it wasn't serious."

"How can an engagement not be serious?"

"When it's arranged by others."

"Oh, I'm dying to hear this one," Mariette said.

Taking a deep breath, he sighed. "All right. My manager—"

"Cantankerous Klaus," Mariette piped in.

"And his partner, Equally-so Ernesto, figures it might be an interesting business move to hook up two of their clients, socially. So, they decided to pair me up with their diva. Some weeks later, our schedules finally allowed us to meet."

"You hadn't met at that point?"

"No. We just knew of each other. So, Klaus and Ernesto finally introduce us, stood back, and waited for the sparks to fly."

"And did they?"

"Oh, yes. Sparks flew. And tempers. And egos. And dishes. We were like two dogs out for each other's blood. They finally pulled us apart after she threatened to smash my hands if I didn't get them off her throat."

Mariette shook her head. "That's totally unbelievable."

Christian laughed. "Why?"

"To begin with, I can't imagine you allowing yourself to be entered into such a contrived arrangement. And I definitely can't imagine you throttling someone."

He shrugged. "I was young and more than a little overwhelmed with myself and my fortuitous life."

"And when was this?"

He flashed his contagious smile. With a glint in his eyes, he said, "Last month."

She laughed. "Come on. This is serious."

"About ten years ago."

"What about since?"

He shook his head. "Too busy working. Believe it or not, I do work. I don't just show up on some stage, play for a couple of hours, and leave. A whole lot of preparation, memorization, and practice goes into what I do. Socializing is something there's not much time for, which was why the arrangement with Lucia seemed like a good idea. At the time."

"Lucia? That's her name?"

He nodded. "Lucia LaTempesta."

"What a pretty name! Lucia LaTempesta. Lucia is 'light.' Tempesta is a 'tempest,' a violent storm. A storm of light."

"She's a violent storm, all right. But I never saw any light."

Mariette couldn't tell from his remarks how Christian felt about the incident. It either had very little impact or a great deal.

Their waiter returned, refilled both wineglasses, and asked, "Was everything all right?"

They both looked down. His plate was pushed to one side, hers to the other. Both plates were barely touched. They looked to each other, guiltily.

"No. Everything's fine. It's just …"

"Just fine, really."

"Shall I remove?" the waiter asked.

They both nodded.

The waiter took the plates away and smiled. "Some things are more important than eating."

They looked at each other and laughed.

"I assume you don't want dessert," she said with a laugh.

"Thank you, I'm fine. It was … just enough."

"I'd like to see that tower up there before it closes."

He came around and pulled out her chair for her. "Certainly."

As they walked the rest of the way up Telegraph Hill, he asked how he could reach her in Ohio.

She gave him an address but said she and Carlotta would be moving shortly. Dormitory life wasn't mandatory after the first year. Besides, they hated it.

She asked how he could be found. Christian handed Mariette a card, saying the best way would be through Klaus. His manager always knew where he would be before he did.

Coit Tower was closed when they arrived. She was disappointed, but he said they'd come back another time.

She started back down. His hand encircled her arm, holding her back. He drew her into the shadows. Surprised by his grasp, she turned to him. Bending forward, his mouth found hers. Her lips were so soft; they seemed to be melting under the heat of his mouth. Her taste and smell filled his senses. He groaned as he felt his tension grow.

Suddenly, his lips enveloped hers. A weakening in her knees and legs was followed by a livening and warmth between her thighs. Falling into his arms, she felt once again their strength and force. The pressure and taste of his mouth thrilled and unnerved her. She flushed rapidly. The suddenness of her bloom weakened her. She swooned.

He pulled back to see Mariette's face. Her cheeks were blushed, her mouth agape and red. He devoured her mouth again, suckling and inhaling her warmth and juices.

The concentrated look in his eyes was black with desire. She wrenched away. Touching the back of her head, she held herself close and laughed nervously. "That's not exactly a brotherly kiss."

"It wasn't meant to be." His voice was hoarse with passion.

"Oh, I thought perhaps you didn't know the difference." An anxious, annoying twitter crept into her voice.

He tried to catch her eye. She kept avoiding his. "I have two brothers. I know the difference."

"Ah, yes, but you see you have no sisters. It's different with girls."

He grasped her shoulders and held them until she looked at him. "Is that what you want of me, Mariette? Brother Christian?"

Her teasing pose dissolved as she looked into his eyes and he looked deeply into hers. "No. It's just that … I dunno."

How vulnerable she looked when she dropped her façade.

He released her shoulders, running his hands down her arms until he caught her wrists. He turned them over and kissed her palms. He knew what "just that" meant. He was twelve years her senior. He would have to wait. She needed time to be a sophomore.

He walked her down the hill to her hotel room and bowed. "I bid you *Auf Wiedersehen.* Do you remember what I told you that means?"

"Good-bye."

"No, it means until I see you again." He gave her a level stare. "And I will see you again. I promise." He walked away without nearly as much resiliency as he thought he had.

Once inside her suite, Mariette waited until she heard Christian leave. Then she reopened the door and hung out the Do Not Disturb sign. Back inside, she quickly stripped off the dress, letting it tumble to the floor. So much for Dragon Lady. She went to the bed and climbed in.

How could she panic at the last minute, pull away, and cast aspersions on his kiss? It made her feel like a tease, playing along and slamming the door in his face at the last minute. She was shocked at herself. That was more Carlotta's style, not hers.

So what went wrong? Why had she done it? She'd been playing along with the innuendos, which was fun, but then what? He started talking about his engagement and that other woman. First, she was incensed and jealous with a woman's pseudo-disdain for "the other woman." And she was scared. It could happen all over again. Her feelings for him could hit her like a sledgehammer. There she'd be with her heart on her sleeve, stuck in Ohio, pining for a man who traveled the world. And this time, there wouldn't be just a couple of floozies in the city. This time, there could be a whole world full of them.

She got up from the bed and picked up the dress. Yes, she'd gotten out just in time. It was time to go home. She put the dress in the bottom of the suitcase and packed everything else on top.

Chapter 9

As soon as Mariette got off the plane, Carlotta was all over her. Carlotta grabbed the onboard luggage from Mariette and escorted her through the Greater Cincinnati International Airport's labyrinth of gates and luggage-retrieval sites.

"Have you lucked out!" Carlotta said. "The registration computer went berserk, and all advance placement in classes got tossed into outer space when some idiot touched the Delete button. I had to hand-pull cards to get us placed in the classes. Fortunately for you, I pulled two sets. So, we're both in sophomore-level nursing with real nursing courses. No more Chem 101 and English Communication. And no more mandatory living in dorms!" Carlotta's dark auburn hair was pulled to one side in a cockeyed ponytail.

Mariette smiled at her friend and put her arms around her. "You're a good friend. And I missed you very much. Thanks for pulling cards for me. How's your appendix?"

"Gone." Carlotta laughed. "Now tell me about the trip."

They watched the bags on the carousel going round and round, occasionally checking one similar to Mariette's.

"It was nice."

"Nice? That's it? Nice."

A blue-plaid suitcase came into view. Mariette reached down and snatched it.

"San Francisco is very beautiful, and the museums are great. I saw El Grecos and Rembrandts and Wyeths. And there was lots of Asian art from all kinds of dynasties. And there's even one of Rodin's *The Thinker* out there."

"So much for places and things. What about people?"

"Pretty much as you'd expect. Cosmopolitan and sophisticated. Fairly distant."

"Did you meet any of them? You know, like men."

Mariette turned away and headed for the exit. "No. I didn't meet anyone."

Carlotta caught up with her. "I swear, 'Ette, without me, you are lost."

Putting down her bag, Mariette turned to Carlotta and hugged her again. "You're right, 'Lotta. I am."

***

It was the sixth time in as many weeks that a big bouquet of flowers arrived at Mariette and Carlotta's apartment in Cincinnati. Carlotta gave the delivery boy fifty cents and brought them in. Before they moved to the apartment, the flowers arrived for Mariette at the dormitory. Usually they were roses, pink ones, but once they were white chrysanthemums.

Carlotta peeked into the box. This time the roses were yellow. "Guess what, 'Ette? Flowers. What a surprise!"

Mariette came into the room and opened the box. Smelling the roses, she smiled. She tossed the previous week's flowers and replaced them with the new ones. "Beautiful color. I love yellow roses." She headed back to their study room.

"Mariette, aren't you forgetting something?" Carlotta followed her.

"What?"

Carlotta thrust the card that was taped to the outside of the box under Mariette's nose. "The card."

Mariette looked at the card from Jerry's Florist. On the outside of the envelope was written: Mariette Stuart. Without opening the envelope, Mariette said, "I know who it's from."

***

Carlotta Mitchell had Mariette Stuart safely tucked into a booth at the Wander Inn. She casually sipped her frozen pineapple daiquiri and offhandedly asked, "So, who's sending the flowers, 'Ette?"

Mariette sipped her diet soda. "Christian Stanislaus."

"Who's he?"

Digging through her purse, Mariette found a business card and handed it to Carlotta. "Someone I met in San Francisco."

"You told me you didn't meet any men."

"I know."

"Are you sure he's the one sending you flowers?"

"Yeah. He's the one who bought me this coat." Mariette pulled up the lapels on the camel hair coat.

"What? You told everyone you won that coat in a drawing at Saks."

"I know, but if I told everyone that some man bought it for me, the first thing they're going to wonder was what I did for it."

"Oh no, 'Ette." Carlotta shook her head. "Everyone knows you're not like that." Carlotta eyed Mariette. She was hurt. Her very best friend had been withholding things from her. She polished off the daiquiri with one noisy slurp and motioned to the waitress for another. "What did you do that he bought the coat?"

"Nothing," Mariette said. "He asked me to leave with him and not pick up my jacket on the way out. I got cold, so he bought me a coat."

The waitress delivered Carlotta's pineapple daiquiri.

Mariette said, "Scotch over, please."

"Weekly flowers and a camel hair coat. I'm getting the distinct impression that this man makes a lot of money—or he just likes spending it. So what does he do for a living?"

"He's a concert pianist."

"Concert pianist! You mean white tie and tails, nine-foot-long grand piano, and a hundred musicians behind him pianist?"

"Well, sometimes he's on stage all alone, but yes, that kind."

Mariette took a sip and then a gulp of the scotch. "He travels the world concertizing, and I'm attracted to him."

"So what's the problem? Is he an oaf? Is he ugly?"

Mariette shook her head. "No, actually, he's quite elegant. Almost too good-looking."

"Mariette, no one is ever *too* good-looking."

"I suppose."

"You got a picture of him?"

"No."

"Didn't you take one?"

"I didn't bring the camera."

"Mariette, you are the only person I know who goes on vacation without a camera." Carlotta's mind worked rapidly as she watched Mariette. "I've got it. The Music Hall. Has he ever played with the Cincinnati Symphony at the Music Hall?"

"I don't know. Maybe. He plays in Europe a lot. Why?"

"Well, if he's played with them, their office might have his picture on file. I think I'll give them a call."

Mariette reached out and grabbed Carlotta's elbow. "No, wait. I've got a better idea." Mariette drained her drink. "Get in the car."

As they drove to the shopping mall, Mariette said, "He was getting ready for a recording session when I saw him.

Maybe there'll be a picture of him on the album or tape or whatever."

Carlotta sank back, enjoying her once bubbly friend, turned phlegmatic since the Robert fiasco, suddenly all aflutter about something or someone.

At the mall, they found a quiet little shop specializing in classical sounds. Mariette walked over to a ladder. Atop it stood a long man with a tiny mustache and a bow tie. She called up to him. "Excuse me, sir? I'm looking for a recording of Rachmaninoff by Christian Stanislaus."

The man's eyes wandered down the shelves until he found the two women at the bottom of his ladder. He watched them for a second or two. "There is no such thing," he said. "Stanislaus has never recorded Rachmaninoff. Others have. Try aisle two. That's composers."

"Well, he would have recorded it this last August."

"It's probably not released yet."

"Would you have—"

The man turned back to sorting his albums. "Aisle one is compiled according to artists. Aisle two is composers."

Mariette headed toward composers. *Who was it Christian said he played? Liszt, of course. He used to swear at him.* It made her chuckle, wondering which of his languages he cursed in.

The pile of record albums for Liszt was huge. She started at the beginning, but when she realized the albums were alphabetized, she flipped to the end. Five albums in, she found *Stanislaus Plays Liszt*. On the cover was a picture of Christian nose to nose with a bust of Liszt. It was an okay picture of Christian as a young man. It was still too stagey though.

"Oh, my goodness!" Carlotta gasped. She came running to Mariette. Shoving an album under Mariette's nose, she demanded, "Is this him? Is this the man who's sending you the flowers?" On the cover, Christian wore a white tie and black tailcoat and leaned back against the side of a Bösendorfer concert grand piano. His arms were folded across his chest, one ankle casually crossed over the other. Looking as if all the world was his, he sported that dazzling smile.

Mariette looked at the picture. "Yeah, that's him."

"Mariette, he's gorgeous. Get in touch with him immediately."

Dazed, Mariette looked at the photo on the cover.

Carlotta shoved the album into Mariette's hands. "Come on, 'Ette. We're taking this with us. Now, let's go."

***

Back at their apartment, Carlotta put the record on the stereo. As Brahms's "Rhapsody in G" played, Mariette sat in the armchair and stared at Christian's picture.

"So, that's why you took an introductory music course this semester, 'Ette," Carlotta said during the first movement. "Well, the music's not particularly my cup of tea, but it sounds as if he knows where all the notes are."

Mariette nodded, dumbly, eyes still on the album cover.

"'Ette. You really ought to call him. Thank him for the flowers."

Mariette had forgotten how rivetingly handsome Christian was and how endearing his smile was.

"I mean, after six weeks, not even a polite acknowledgment or a 'buzz off, jerk.' He's going to think you're uncouth."

Mariette hadn't forgotten. She'd put it out of her mind or tried to, but images of Christian kept sneaking back to her at the oddest times. In the shower—or during an IV demonstration in class—she heard his laugh and saw his face. And now, Carlotta was lining up with her anxious thoughts.

"'Ette, are you on this planet? Don't you think you should give him a call?"

"I don't know where he is," she fired back.

"You've got his card. The phone number's on it."

"That's just his manager's office. He's probably off in Switzerland or somewhere. His manager probably is too. The number's probably just an answering service."

"And you're not going to answer the *probablys* until you call to find out."

Mariette flapped her hands to shoo Carlotta away. "Get away from me, Carlotta. Leave me alone."

Carlotta backed off. Whatever this man had done or hadn't done, it certainly shook Mariette from her torpor. Now, if she would just not fight it, maybe Carlotta would get the old 'Ette back, rather than the basket case Robert left in his wake.

***

Left alone, Mariette listened to Christian's music pouring through the speakers. As the playing continued, Mariette became more agitated. During Christian's fervent attack on the Animato movement of Liszt's "La Campanella," something within her burst. Suddenly, she was riddled with anger. Welled-up fury that had seethed for two years erupted. She banged her fists on the arms of the chair and cursed. *Damn him!* Wasn't it bad enough Robert had crushed her dreams of love and marriage until death do us part? Whatever happened to that saucy young girl who loved and embraced life?

Mariette thought back to her last three days in San Francisco. Her mind unwound the events: pouring out her past to Christian at Fisherman's Wharf, revealing her secret dream of studying oceanography at the Japanese Tea Garden, and finally his rescuing her at Ocean Beach. So many things happened with that man in such a short time. And they were things of import—not things packed away and forgotten like cheap souvenirs from a summer fling.

During Chopin's "Revolutionary Étude," Christian's heartened playing emblazoned Mariette. What had Christian said at the Japanese Tea Garden? "Believe in yourself. I do." Mariette's fingers gently caressed Christian's photo on the album cover. And he'd also said, "Risk it. I dare you." She answered the photo. "Okay, Player. You're on." She got up, ran to the telephone, and punched in the phone number on Christian's business card.

A woman answered the phone. "Steiner & Ernesto International, San Francisco office. May I help you?"

Taking a deep breath, Mariette said, "My name is Mariette Stuart. Is this where I can reach Christian Stanislaus?"

"We do represent Mr. Stanislaus. If this is a business matter, I can help you."

"Well, actually, it's personal."

"For personal matters, you may write him in care of—what did you say your name was?"

"Stuart. Mariette Stuart."

There was a gasp on the other end of the line. "Hold on," said the woman. "Papa! Line one. Pick it up. It's her!" Then the phone receiver was muffled.

The next voice Mariette heard was deep, male, lightly accented, and angry.

"Fraulein Stuart, this is Klaus Steiner. *Bitte*! Please! Reply to Krischan. Either a valentine or a rejection will do. He thrives on heightened emotion, so either is fine, but the limbo you have him in now? He's driving me and the staff *verrückt*, you know, crazy."

"Papa!" the woman shouted.

Again the receiver was smothered. When the man's voice came back on the line, its acerbity was replaced with soft, luring tones.

"Fraulein Stuart. *Entschuldigen Sie bitte!*"

The woman in the background said, "He begs you're pardon. He's sorry."

"I'm sorry, Fraulein. My daughter just informed me that I'm being irascible and living up to Krischan's little sobriquet of me."

Mariette burst out laughing. "You mean Cantankerous Klaus?"

"*Ja.*" The man's chortling was hearty and infectious. "He's told you that, has he?"

"Really, Mr. Steiner. Excuse me, Herr Steiner. It's my fault. I called at the wrong time. I should have waited until tomorrow morning. That's Wednesday and all—"

"Fraulein, pardon my interruption, but why is Wednesday better?"

"Well, that's the day … you know … you see your friend and all. And you're more receptive. And jovial. And …"

"Krischan told you I'm in a better mood after I see Rosa?" Klaus guffawed. "So, that's why he's always sure to check in Wednesday mornings. I've wondered. It sounds like he's told you a great many things, hasn't he?"

"Well, yeah, I guess. I mean he is nice to talk with. He's clever. Funny. Wise." She shook her head. "But why am I telling you this? You must know all that."

"No, Fraulein. I don't. As his impresario, in Krischan, I only see an artist with all the self-absorption of the very talented. Distracted and always focusing on something just past my head. That he talks to you and you enjoy it, I applaud. It sounds as if you've turned a reticent man quite *gesprä'chig*. You know, gabby. Now, concerning what I said before about responding to Krischan, you do what's right for you. He's a big boy; he can handle whatever it will be."

"No, Herr Steiner. I do want to respond. Where is he? Is he in this country?"

"No, he's not in this country. Just a second. *Bitte!*" Klaus called out. "Grete, *wo ist Krischan?*" When he came back on, he was positively chatty. "My daughter is asking her computer where Krischan is at this moment. She has decided we cannot possibly go into the future without a computer. So, she spends all of her time putting information in and taking it out. Her mother did better with a booklet and pencil. Ah, he's in Zurich. Tonight, he plays at Tonhalle. Tomorrow, he travels to Strasbourg."

"Is there any way I can get in touch with him?"

"I don't think so." Klaus Steiner pulled a package of walnuts from his jacket pocket and popped one into his mouth. "With the time difference, he'd be on stage right now, or just finishing. Afterward, he'll probably go straight to Strasbourg. He likes traveling after a concert when he's all worked up, but you could try. Let me pass you over to my daughter. Grete will give you names and numbers of places where he will be."

"Danke, Herr Steiner!"

Klaus laughed. "You're welcome. Thank you for calling. It's been a delight. Auf Wiedersehen, Fraulein Stuart."

There was a click, and the woman's voice came back on the line. "Fraulein Stuart, this is Grete Steiner."

"Hello. Please call me Mariette."

"Hello, Mariette. And I am Grete. Let me see now. It's 2:30 p.m. here in San Francisco. So it's 11:30 p.m. in Zurich. Christian might still be registered at Helmhaus, or he might have already checked out and be on his way."

"Excuse me, Grete?"

"*Ja.*"

A disturbing thought struck Mariette. "Does Christian do this all the time? Not the traveling, I mean, but, the long-distance sending of flowers to women."

"Krischan? Goodness, no! If he did, I'd certainly refuse to be a party to it. Fortunately, he doesn't go in for playing around. Some of our other artists like fooling around with stage-door groupies, but Krischan's a bit of a monk. I don't mind the bother."

In the background, Mariette could hear the rapid operation of a computerized printer that was whirring as fast as her mind.

"I even tease him about it," Grete continued. "Bruder Krischan married only to his piano," Grete guffawed. "Mariette, I'm sending a copy of his itinerary for the next few weeks. You should be able to reach him somewhere along the line. And, of course, I'll tell him you've called when he checks in tomorrow. Is there a place where I can fax this to you?"

When the conversation ended, Mariette hung up the phone. She'd done it. She was jubilant, but a part of her wondered what she had done. She looked at the yellow roses in the vase. She was getting in contact with the man to thank him for the flowers he'd sent. Mariette shook her head. No, that wasn't all. That was what the cautious part wanted her to think. The saucy part was doing what was right for her.

***

Christian Stanislaus was not registered in the hotel where Grete said he'd be. Mariette didn't know enough German to ask the front desk if they knew whether he was in town or not. Instead, she tried Grete's alternative approach. She'd write a letter to Christian and send it to the Continental Hotel in Munich. He'd be there for five days the following week. In the meantime, he could just know that she'd been in touch with his manager's office when he called in on Wednesday.

Mariette took out a blank sheet of paper and stared at Christian's picture on the album. After all this time, she couldn't think of what she wanted to say. However, she could think of what she wanted to do. She wanted to kiss him in that dizzying way he'd kissed her on Telegraph Hill. Finally, she scribbled on the paper: "Thanks for the flowers. Cheers, Mariette."

His reply came by express mail. It was a copy of the photo used for his album. In the corner, it was signed: "To Mariette. Best regards, Christian Stanislaus. Regrettably crisscrossing every continent but yours."

She faxed him back: "You 'Chris-cross' this way Christmas week. You're playing the Music Hall in Cincinnati on December 19. You're a last-minute fill-in courtesy of Grete Steiner. See you then, Player."

He replied with a box of chocolates and a note: "Bless Grete, the little busybody. I'll tell her to leave your name at the Music Hall box office to get you in. Keep well. Over time and distance. CS, the piano player."

Chapter 10

Mariette Stuart finished her last exam at eleven o'clock on December 20. She was exuberant. Classes were over for the year, vacation was starting, and she pulled open the door of the study hall and peeked out.

Out in the hallway, Christian Stanislaus was looking around and biding his time. He looked resplendent in a dark gray three-piece business suit, white broadcloth shirt, and pale blue silk tie.

Mariette waited until Christian's back was turned. Then she swept into the hallway, ran up from behind, and grabbed his hand. "Come on," she said.

As they fled up the corridor, he said, "Where are we going?"

"To my car."

"Oh!" Christian tried slowing the pace to get a look at Mariette's face. "Hello."

Her pace only quickened. They left the building and headed for the parking lot.

"Hello! How was your concert?"

"Fine."

"Don't be angry. I couldn't make it. I was studying for finals."

"Oh, good."

Christian's surprised delight shocked Mariette. "Good? If I were you, I'd be livid. You left me tickets and everything."

He shrugged. "There's plenty of time. How did your finals go?"

"I think I aced them. What did you play?"

"'Emperor Concerto.' When do you find out about your grades?"

"January 18. Oh, I love that piece. Sorry I missed it."

He smiled. "Don't be. There'll be other times."

Mariette pulled Christian to a halt beside her blue Mustang. Opening the trunk, she pulled out a pair of black high-heeled shoes and traded her white nurse's oxfords for them. She started unbuttoning her nurse's uniform.

Mouth dropping open, Christian slowly shook his head. "Whoa!"

Mariette disrobed to reveal a soft floral jersey dress hugging her body. She tossed in the uniform and slammed the lid.

"No!" Christian protested. "I wasn't complaining. Don't let me stop you."

Mariette stopped jostling. "I was only getting rid of the wretched uniform. Nothing else is coming off."

"I thought you were getting an uncontrollable urge to defrock."

Mariette tossed her head. "My uncontrollable urges will come later. Now get in my car."

A dark swarthy man of medium height walked up to the car next to Mariette's. As she walked over to the passenger's side to let in Christian, the man said, "Well, good day, Miss Stuart." Smile plastered on his face, the man eyed Mariette up and down. "All through with finals?"

"Good morning, Mr. Bulter. Yes, just through."

Bulter didn't get in his car. He stood with his arms folded in front of Mariette's passenger door and watched Christian.

"Oh! Mr. Bulter, this is Christian Stanislaus. Christian, this is my music teacher, Mr. Bulter."

"Geoffrey," Bulter added.

Christian extended his hand. "Geoffrey, it's nice to—" Christian's hand jerked back, touching his chin while his brow furrowed. He pointed at Bulter. "We've met before."

The smile still chiseled on Geoffrey's face turned sickly. Bulter deferred, shaking his head. "I'm sure a man of your notoriety meets many people."

Christian's face eased as the memory dawned. "Yorkshire. Ten years ago. We played off each other in the Leeds Competition."

Bulter bristled. "Very good! You have an infallible memory. Of course that doesn't necessarily help one's playing. Does it? The music critic in the *Bee* really slaughtered your performance last night."

"Did he?" Christian replied. "I wouldn't know. I never read music critics." He shrugged. "What's the point? I know if my performance is good or not."

Mariette suppressed a giggle. She was sure she heard the gnashing of Geoffrey Bulter's teeth.

Christian's smile continued to light his face. "So, what are you doing now, Geoffrey. Still playing the circuit?"

"No, I'm in the music department here. I teach coeds, like Miss Stuart, music appreciation."

Christian looked around. "Teaching on a beautiful pastoral campus? Oh, I envy you that."

"I'll bet you do."

Bowing his head, Christian turned to Mariette. "Especially those attended by such stunning coeds as Mariette."

"And how do you know Miss Stuart?"

Mariette and Christian exchanged embarrassed smiles and an awkward moment of silence. Then Christian turned back to Bulter and whispered, "Old family friend. My family and hers are like that." He held up two fingers close together. "She's like a sister to me."

On cue, Mariette slipped her hand through the crook in Christian's arm. "Come on, dear brother, or you'll miss your plane." She opened the car door and turned back to Bulter. "He's off to Frankfurt. Has a recital at Hessische-Rundfunk on Saturday." She helped Christian into the car and waved. "Have a good vacation, Mr. Bulter."

Geoffrey Bulter watched Mariette and Christian drive away. *Geoffrey Bulter loathed Christian Stanislaus. Christian Stanislaus got the Leeds and the International Franz Liszt Piano Competition prizes away from Bulter. Geoffrey Bulter wanted to destroy Christian Stanislaus.*

"She's like a sister to me." *Bollocks! He's banging her. So, Christian Stanislaus likes Mariette Stuart. We'll see what we can do about that.*

Mariette barely had the car started before she broke into gales of laughter. "You know him," she squealed. "You even scored a competition over him. No wonder he went into an acid-spitting tirade when I mentioned your name in class once." Ramming the gears into reverse, Mariette jerked the car from its parking place, laughing all the while.

Chapter 11

Elbow rested on the top of his car seat, Christian watched Mariette as she maneuvered the car. Now that she was seated, he could feast his eyes on her haunting face. Her raven black hair had grown long, down to her shoulders. It was soft and feminine. Her eyes sparkled with a hint of mischief. He thought he remembered how beautiful she was, but his memory paled in comparison to the real thing. "Why? What did he say?"

Putting the car into gear, she peeled out of the parking lot. "All hype. No talent."

Christian crumpled and grasped his stomach, gasping. "Ow. That one hurts."

She pulled onto Vine Street and laughed again. "You don't give a hoot what he says."

Christian sat up. "You're right. I don't."

"You know that paper he was talking about? It's the college rag. The music critic calls himself Euterpe. That's a pseudonym for Geoffrey Bulter."

"That's why I never read critics. Most often, what they write has nothing to do with my playing and a lot to do with their politics." He looked out the window, trying to figure out where they were going. "Euterpe, hmm? One of the Muses, I believe. Clever little handle. Better than the Shark. That's how he referred to himself in Yorkshire." They appeared to be heading downtown. "He used to act like one too. Preyed on all he viewed as weaker than himself. Always trying to intimidate and disrupt." Christian shook his head. "There's enough pressure in those competitions. Creating more does not help."

A look of wicked glee filled Mariette's eyes. "Did you absolutely cream the bum in Yorkshire?"

"Not only did I cream him in Yorkshire—I made goulash out of him in Budapest."

Mariette cackled with delight. "Good! Serves him right, the sanctimonious bastard. I thought he was probably a jerk."

"He's not a jerk; he's a shark. And that's how he plays. Only instead of going into a feeding frenzy, he goes into a mindless playing frenzy."

"You nearly sent him to the floor when you told him you envied his teaching position."

"I meant that. That's what I'll do eventually."

"Teach? You're kidding."

"No, that's my next step. I'm not going to chase my tail all over the world for the rest of my life. I've already *seen*. Now, I'm *doing*. The next step is to teach. That's where I can learn the most and really make the piano mine." He turned toward Mariette. "Where are we going?"

"Your hotel."

"Why?"

"Because I just finished the most grueling semester I've ever had. Now I want to go to a nice fancy downtown bar and have a drink. The hotel you are staying at has a good one." She pulled the car into the hotel parking area. "Come on."

At the entrance to the bar, Mariette gave the room a cursory glance and put her hands on Christian's arm. "It's too crowded. Can we go up to your room and have them send it up?"

Christian walked into the bar and looked around. One couple was huddled in the far corner of the room. Christian wondered about the girl poised on his arm. "Sure."

In the elevator, he watched Mariette pace, her dress swirling around her. She grinned at him and tossed her head; he turned away. He'd swear she was on the make. He felt himself tighten. What was he doing going up to his hotel room with a woman who could be playfully seductive one minute only to panic and pull back the next? He didn't need that again. Last time, it had taken him days to shake the morosity the encounter had left him in.

He walked over to the railing of the glass-enclosed elevator and gripped it as his gaze fell to the atrium below. It was not the time to let his hormones run rampant. They'd have one drink in his room and leave. That's all.

Mariette watched Christian, enjoying his nervousness.

Dropping the key twice, Christian finally got the door opened. His suite was complete with a wet bar, a whirlpool bath, and a fireplace.

"Wow!" Mariette slipped off her shoes and wriggled her toes in the dark green, deep-cut rug. "Holy smokes. You always get rooms like this?"

Christian watched Mariette's pink shell-like toes caress the rug. Hurriedly, he turned and went straight to the bar. "No. But when I stay at the same hotel chain often enough, I'm occasionally upgraded to something like this. I gather Grete's been saving the upgrades."

Mariette prowled around the suite. "Well, my regards to Grete." She swept back into the room. "There's even a phone in the bathroom. You can talk while you whirlpool."

"And pray you don't electrocute yourself when it falls in." His voice was stiff, sarcasm unnatural. "What are you drinking?"

As she moved in closer, Mariette saw he was trembling. Hopefully, he was suffering the same discomfort she was. Her head leaned around his arm, looking up at his face. "What are you making?"

"Something simple," he said. "Whiskey on the rocks or a gin and tonic I can handle. Maybe even fake a martini. But if you want a margarita or a mai tai or something, I have to call down to the bar."

She sashayed over to the elevated hearth and hopped up on the firestone that jutted from it. As she sat, she crossed her legs. Her dress crept up to her thighs. "Scotch over. What kind of scotch?"

He read the courtesy bottles on the shelf over the bar. "Dewar's or Crown Royal."

"Crown Royal's Canadian whiskey. I'll take the Dewar's please."

With cramped, jerky moves, Christian packed crushed ice into a glass. Gone were his usual flowing rhythms. He tried to measure an ounce of scotch. Not coordinating bottle spout to shot glass, he gave up and poured the liquor directly over the ice. Christian stood with his back to the bar, keeping the distance between them. He leaned forward to hand her the drink.

Flashing a playful grin, Mariette let her fingers linger over his before taking hold of the glass.

Christian pulled his hand back as if stung. Quickly, he turned around and gripped the bar.

"Uh-oh," Mariette said.

He pivoted back. "What's wrong?"

With the glass held up to eye level, her index finger beckoned him. "Come here."

"What is it? What happened? Are you all right?"

She pointed to the glass and gestured again. "You gotta see this."

He watched her as he walked over. Her eyes were still intent on the glass, and her smile showed her dimples. "What are you seeing?"

One more wiggle of her finger got him to bend forward, his head at her level. She put down the glass and encircled her arms around his neck, flicking her tongue over his lips. His mouth opened in surprise. The kiss was warm, juicy, and deep—and every bit as dizzying as that kiss on Telegraph Hill.

Yanking from her, Christian held up both hands. "Don't start with me, Mariette. Unless you're ready to finish it."

His fury was delicious. "Well, it's about time you got the message. I've practically had to drag you up to your own hotel room." She egged him on some more. "You know what your problem is, Player? You're too much of a gentleman." Turning her back, she reached for her drink. Before she could, she was lifted in his arms and cradled against his chest. Carting her to the bed, he tossed her down on pillows and comforters.

Her protest was interspersed with laughter. "My drink."

"No. Alcohol deadens sensations. And I want you to feel it all. Now, look at me."

He was leaning over her, hands planted on either side of her head. Her eyes wandered up to the buttons of his vest and the knot in his silk tie. She looked into his face. He was glaring down at her with fixed intent. The instantaneous change in him was shocking. His eyes were black with passion. She'd seen it before at Fisherman's Wharf and at the Japanese Tea Garden. When he spoke of his music, his eyes darkened with yearning and lust. And now they were focused on her. Fascinated, she couldn't withdraw from their lure.

"Watch me."

His hands went to the sash of her dress, and it was no longer tied. His fingers stroked under her chin; her eyes closed to the feathery sensation. She felt his hand brush down her neck. When he paused at the first button of her dress, she opened her eyes. His stare was still riveted on her. A brief glance down instructed her to watch his hands. Her eyes strayed from his, traveling to his fingers as they slipped the first button from its hole. The other buttons' undoing rapidly followed. He eased back the cloth, and with a gentle touch, he caressed the exposed area. To her brassiere's front closure, he bent down and softly blew. She looked from his hands into his eyes. He was staring into hers. Holding her gaze, he snapped loose the bra's constriction. Her breasts swelled from their enclosure. With a heavy groan, he bent to them. His mouth touched her breasts; her nipples responded, forming tight little mounds.

"Ah, perfect," he whispered.

He savored her breasts as his light touch stroked her inner thigh.

She panted as warm rushes of blood surged through her limbs.

His assault on her breasts ceased as quickly as it started. She cried out at the loss. Her gaze once again was caught in thrall as he slipped the stockings and panties from her in one swift move. His hands deftly stroked her inner thighs. Her eyes closed in pleasure. His fingers started nimble little forays, circling ever deeper between her legs. Tickling and petting, his touch only reached so far. Each time, he teased a little further—and pulled back. Once, he stopped altogether. She moaned in frustration as her tension eased.

Suddenly, his bare chest was on hers. It was ecstasy. The touch of his skin quenched her ragged nerves. She wanted the arms that bound her never to unclench. As she became aware of that, he pulled away, kissing a trail down her breastbone to her navel. There, he looked up at her with eyes so mesmerizing.

She reached out for him.

He pulled up alongside her. Hungrily, his mouth encircled hers. His tongue thrust through her lips. While tasting her mouth inside and out, his hand traveled deeper and deeper through her thighs. He touched where her tensions were paramount. His fingers were slowly rubbing and caressing, creating rhythms and playing with them. They caused a fiery urgency within her like she'd never known.

The sensations he provoked panicked her. She knew what he was trying to do, but it wasn't going to work. It never did. It just frustrated her.

Gasping, she pulled her mouth from his. "I don't think—"

"No! Don't think!" he demanded. "Feel!"

All at once, she felt his mouth, hands, and fingers everywhere. The surprise of his touch in new places spiraled her higher. The confusion of where the feeling would occur next, the surprise of a feathery caress or a heavy satisfying stroke, overwhelmed her. Her urgency rose, peaked, and spilled over.

Her rapture cascaded, almost flowing away. Suddenly, she felt him deep within her. The pressure was hard and gratifying, and she wanted more. She captured his mouth with hers. Deep within her, she squeezed—needing more and more ecstasy. Her rapid compressions sent them both up and over the summit, tumbling down the other side.

His body went limp upon release and collapsed on the bed. Stunned, Mariette watched in disbelief. His strangled cries of passion had thrilled her, but now his breathlessness and immobility scared her. What had she done? Instinctively, she touched his throat to check for a pulse. Abruptly, he took a full breath and exhaled a low, satisfied growl. Enveloping her in his arms, he nestled her close.

She rested her head on his chest and snuggled in. Her body relaxed as she stared into space. *It's finally happened,* she thought. *After all this time, it's finally happened. It was as thrilling as it was alleged to be. Heavens, it was darned near mystical!* She took a deep breath and exhaled slowly. "Whew!"

Looking down at their sprawling bodies, she smiled. She had been too preoccupied at the time. In fact, she didn't even remember him disrobing. But if he hadn't looked elegant in his underwear, he certainly looked beautiful in his altogether. She pulled away and raised herself on an elbow to get a better view.

His long legs were muscular. His chest was powerfully built. His upper torso and wide shoulders tapered to a taut gut. So this was the human machine with the strength to pull her from the ocean's depths and the tenderness to raise her to ecstatic heights? She bent forward and blew at the forest of tawny brown hair on his chest.

Roused, he glanced at her. "Give me just a few minutes, Liebchen. Then, I'll be with you."

She wanted to stay with him, but she was too energized to stay put. She had to move. He didn't stir when she slipped off the bed. She sneaked into the bathroom and filled the tub.

From the whirlpool bath, Mariette listened to Christian's heavy breathing as he snoozed. More than anything, she wanted to tell the world the wondrous thing that had just happened to her. She kept glancing at the phone. She could call Carlotta, but if she did, his prediction would no doubt come true. Her grip on the phone would weaken just as she got to the juicy parts, and the receiver would drop into the water. Mariette chuckled at the imagined scene of Christian waking up to find a boiled woman in his tub.

She shook her head to chase the ghoulish thoughts away. Besides, what was so marvelous that she needed to share it with anyone? She'd been married before. It was no doubt assumed

Robert had fulfilled her, but that was dead wrong. Robert only climbed aboard, satisfied himself, and rolled off. Like some kid who put a coin in a mechanical horse, when his quarter ran out, he took off. She'd come to believe satisfaction from a man just wasn't possible for her.

Adjusting the whirlpool jets to focus between her legs, Mariette sighed. Well, Player just exploded that belief. This time, making love was different. His total attention had been on her, and she'd responded like a crocus in the spring. Her screams were joyous; her writhing was satisfying. Her body still surged with the afterglow. Damn, she wanted to shout it from the rooftops!

The unmistakable pop of a champagne cork sounded behind her. A flute of champagne passed over her head and appeared before her eyes.

She reached up for the glass. "Thank you."

Christian walked around into view. "No. Thank you."

Their eyes met, and they gazed at each another. She sat rosy and glistening as the water swirled around her. He stood proud and awed, like a man who'd unearthed a fabled treasure.

She raised her glass to him. "To mutual gratitude."

He clinked his glass to hers. "To newfound joy."

He sat on the tub's edge. Timidly, he reached out a well-muscled hand and touched her breast as if it were the thinnest of porcelain. Closing his eyes, he shook his head. In a guttural growl, he said. "Mariette, you are so lovely."

"It was never like that for me before," she said.

"Me neither."

She contemplated his face. It was nice of him to say that, but she didn't believe him. He knew too much of life, much too much not to have those experiences come along all the time.

"Personally, I'm famished," he said. "How about you?"

"Ditto."

"Would you like to go out to eat or would you prefer I call room service?"

"Right now, I can't think of anywhere more enticing than here."

"Enticing. Nice choice of words." He stood. "I'll get the menu. We can call from here."

Mariette stood and reached for a towel to wrap herself.

At the doorway, he turned back. "Don't get up. I don't want to spoil this vision."

"I'm going to get wrinkly if I stay here much longer."

"Oh, all right. Don't want a soggy woman on my hands."

She pulled the wet towel from around her and threw it at him.

He caught it with one hand and smiled.

After supper—with bodies fed and heads intoxicated with wine and each other—they drifted off to sleep, wrapped in each other's arms.

Chapter 12

At four o'clock, the phone rang. Christian fumbled for it.

"Ja, Stanislaus."

"Good morning, Mr. Stanislaus. This is your wake-up call."

"*Danke! Sag-en Sie mir bitte …* wait a minute." The voice had spoken English, which was his cue to reply in kind. "Could you please tell me the day, the date, and where I am?"

Mariette opened her eyes and watched.

"This is Friday, December 21, in beautiful downtown Cincinnati."

"Cincinnati. In Ohio?"

"Cincinnati. Ohio. United States of America. North American continent. Planet Earth."

Christian chuckled. "Oh, yes. Earth. That's in the Milky Way, isn't it? Nice little blue-green planet. I think I have my coordinates pinpointed now. And with whom am I discoursing?"

"Earth man Stephen Smith."

"Thank you, Stephen. You woke me with a smile."

He hung up the phone and rolled back under the covers.

Mariette said, "You didn't know where you were?"

"Oh, I'm sorry, Liebchen. I didn't mean for my call to wake you. Go back to sleep."

"You wake up in bed with a woman—and you don't know where you are?"

"No, I knew exactly where I was and with whom. It's just force of habit. I'm always waking up in a strange bed. It's disorienting. Rather than going through several blank minutes of where I laid my head down last, I just ask whoever wakes me the day, the date, and where I am. It's easier than pretending I know and sneaking looks at newspapers and telephone books to get a hint."

She had no idea if he was serious or not, but the thought of his scrambling for newspapers and phone books to determine his whereabouts tickled her.

He bent forward and kissed her. "I've got to pack and get ready. Why don't you grab some more sleep?"

"You mind if I stay here and watch you?"

He went over to the chest of drawers. "Suit yourself."

"Well, some people don't like being stared at. I know it makes me nervous."

He talked as he pulled open drawers, leaving out the ones that were filled. "Mariette, thousands of people watch me every week. If that bothers me, then I'm in the wrong business."

Mariette chuckled. All it needed was a rim shot on snare drum for an ending. "From what you said yesterday, it sounds as if you're intent on switching businesses." She tried to picture him on a college campus. In a classroom. Chalk dust on his pants and hands. No, Christian would never look like the rumpled specimens of education she knew.

"You mean the teaching? Yes, someday."

She rolled over on her stomach and put her chin on her fist as she followed his movements. "When?"

He finished putting his socks in the suitcase. His gaze drifted to the ceiling. "August 24, 2000, 9:00 a.m."

It would be like him to be so precise. "Where?"

"Now, that's a little vague."

She guffawed. He was preening for her. She loved it and fed him another straight line. "Why do you put away your clothes in hotel-room drawers when you are only going to be here a day or two? I spent two weeks in San Francisco, and I lived out of the suitcase the entire time."

"And you never felt at home, did you?"

"In a hotel room in San Francisco? No. Too exotic."

"Well, my home travels around. It gives me a sense of belonging and some permanence if I put everything in drawers when I first arrive and pack it all up when I leave. It gives me a sense of home."

"Oh, that makes sense." She kicked her legs back and forth. He'd just fed her back the straight line. "Of course when the front-desk clerk rings in the morning, you have to ask him where that home is."

"Don't tempt me with your beguiling ways, woman. If I don't focus on this plane I have to catch, I'll wind up in bed with you all day."

She sighed. "A fate worse than death."

"A fate I'd die for." Turning to her, he bowed. "Now, you'll have to excuse me, Liebchen. I have ablutions to perform."

Mariette watched him leave the room. Water in the bathroom sink sounded. She rolled over and laughed. Nobody she knew "performed ablutions." Being with him was like living in a nineteenth-century novel. He even dressed the part. His tailcoat and trousers, covered in suffocating cleaner's plastic, were hanging on the door hook. She went to them. Too bad she hadn't seen him in them. He'd been quite gracious about her not attending his concert. Funny how that sort of thing wasn't important to him. Most men she knew were dying for the woman to understand and appreciate what they did for a living.

Mariette's hand wriggled underneath the plastic and caressed the wool tailcoat with its satin-trimmed lapels. She was sure he looked quite the gentleman in it. *Oh no*, she thought, *wrong word. Oh, yes,* her body recalled, *right word.* She would have to keep mindful of his impulsive reaction when accused of being one. She definitely wanted to use it again.

She heard the water in the basin turn off and the shower turn on. Oh, she wished he wasn't leaving. It was too soon, much too soon. She needed time to wallow in these newfound desires with him.

Tiptoeing to the bathroom door, she peeked in. She could see his body's outline behind the shower curtain. Shedding his T-shirt that she'd slept in, she glimpsed behind the curtain.

***

Palms pressed against the wall behind the showerhead, Christian leaned into the water, blasting his face. His sinuses were killing him. The pressure was brutal. He couldn't breathe. Even his voice was annoyingly nasal. An antihistamine would clear it, but it would also make him lose his focus and haze his judgment. He needed his concentration intact.

Without warning, two soft mounds of flesh pressed into his back. He slowly lifted his face from the water surge. A terry cloth towel started rubbing circles on his right shoulder. It proceeded across the blade to his spine.

"Stop!" he ordered. "Right there."

The scrubbing stopped.

"Now, down a little and to the left."

Mariette laughed. She finished rubbing that spot and moved on.

He tried turning around, but she stopped him.

"I haven't finished back here. Control yourself."

Leaning into the water's flow, he relished the luxury of having his back rubbed. Oh, he did lose control with this woman, and it was not unpleasant. Standing still until he could no longer, he turned and pulled her to him.

Their kiss lifted her off the ground—or maybe that was him. She neither knew nor cared.

He turned off the water and wrapped her in his robe. Scooping her up, he carried her kicking and protesting back to the bedroom.

"I was in the midst of doing something in there," she said.

"Now, we're in the middle of doing something in here."

Carefully unwrapping his treasure, he proceeded to examine the fine details. Her dainty waist was small enough that he could completely encircle it with his hands. The shapely curve of her thighs and the muscles that flowed from her hips to her knees made him groan and reach for her.

Chapter 13

Rivaling the previous night's performance, Mariette once again scaled heights she never thought possible. When she reached for him to share in her joy, he pulled back.

"No, my dear," he said. "For all the times that never were, this time's just yours."

She looked into the handsome face looking down on her. So he did know her responses were brand-spanking-new. Did he also realize these sensations were becoming rapidly addictive?

The phone rang, pulling him from her. He leaned over and picked it up. "Stanislaus."

She couldn't hear the other end this time and was too dreamy to care.

"Hello, Stephen. Yes, I know I have 9:05. Yes, it is 7:00 and the height of commute hour ... I'm on my way down ... limousine to air service? Just a second. Maybe not." He turned to her. "Would it be possible for you to drive me to the airport?"

Mariette sat up aghast. "Of course I'm driving you to the airport. Isn't that why I'm up here to begin with?"

He shook his head.

"You're right. My motives were ulterior."

He nodded.

"No, Stephen, I won't need a ride to the airport. I have one. And, yes, I'm on my way down to check out. *Danke.*" He hung up the phone. "My motives were ulterior too." He leaned down and kissed her. "They have been ever since you asked me if Liszt ever cursed back." He kissed her again and went off to dress.

"Player, I don't want to leave you."

He watched her in the mirror as he knotted his tie. It hit him in a flash. Why not have her travel with him? It certainly wasn't uncommon. In fact, most performers had entire entourages with them. He didn't because it wasn't his preference, but that could change. "You're on vacation now, aren't you?"

She shook the wrinkles from her jersey dress and wrapped it around herself. "For about a month, yeah."

It was perfect. They could celebrate Christmas Eve in Bavaria, go to Vienna, and waltz in the New Year at the Emperor's Ball in the Hofburg. Yes! If he couldn't get her a seat on the flight he was taking out, he'd get her a seat on another one.

His eyes went back and forth between her reflection in the mirror and the knotting of his tie. "Got a passport?"

She shook her head and sighed. "No."

He finished the Windsor knot and his dream. Without a passport, she couldn't even board the plane. "Get one. You'll need it. It can take a while—sometimes months—depending on the backlog."

He put on his jacket and grabbed his suitcase.

She took his garment bag, and they walked out the door.

In the elevator, he held her hand. "There are so many places in the world I want to show you, Mariette."

In the lobby, he checked out while she retrieved her car.

Mariette pulled her car onto I-275 and headed for the airport. She could feel Christian's eyes on her as she drove.

"I don't know when I'll be back in the country," he said. "I'll have Grete send you my itinerary."

"She already has. You play Symphony Hall in San Diego on January 20."

"Close." He nodded to her. "Only a couple thousand miles from Cincinnati."

"Yes, but only a couple from University of California at San Diego in La Jolla."

"Am I playing La Jolla too?"

"No. I am. They've just accepted my transfer. Or they will if I didn't botch up the microbiology exam. That was the one I was studying for on the night of your concert."

He watched her face closely and tried to decipher the message in what she was saying. "Does UC–San Diego have a nursing department?"

"No, but it has Scripps Institution of Oceanography. I've been accepted—contingent upon my final grades."

"Well!" He leaned over and kissed her cheek. "Congratulations! I'm very happy for you. As I'm sure are all the fish in the sea."

"You should be. You're the one who said you knew I could do it."

"Yes, I knew you could do it. But I didn't know if you would. That was strictly up to you."

"Then stop beaming like you just gave birth."

Mariette pulled her car into the parking garage, and they headed off to Terminal C. At the metal detector, Christian breezed through. Mariette tried twice, shedding various metal objects the scanner found offensive.

In the waiting area, Mariette and Christian clung to each other. There was so much to say in such very little time, yet there was nothing to say at all.

When the flight attendant announced early boarding for Christian's flight, Mariette looked up at him anxiously.

Christian shook his head.

"Not just yet. Women with babies and elderly board first."

She hung on him. "Player, don't go."

He held her in his arms.

"Mariette, don't ask me that. Please. The way I feel now—standing here, half-drunk in love with you—I'll do it. I'll run away with you as if nothing else in the world mattered, but it does. I need our relationship to be more than passion, no matter how intense that is. I need this to turn into a lifetime and not just a torrid six-month affair. Fleeing with you won't make that happen. Please understand."

She watched his beautiful face as he beseeched her so eloquently. The pleading in his eyes reaffirmed the power he said she held over him.

Final boarding was called, but he held her in his arms, awaiting her words.

She talked within herself. *The time to decide is now. What is it to be, biding my time for a long haul of lonesome waiting or the immediate satisfaction of having him near?* With a ragged sigh, she backed from the cheap victory. Hugging him, she whispered, "Go well, Player. Go well."

Trembling, he turned and walked to the gate. At the doorway, he stopped for a torturous second. Then straightening himself, he went on without looking back.

Though she needed one last glimpse of his face, she understood he couldn't do so.

Mariette watched the plane take off. When she could see it no longer, she walked to the airport bar. But for cocktail waitresses huddled at one end, the bar was empty. It was barely nine thirty.

Waiting for the bartender, she thought of what Christian said about alcohol deadening the senses and his wanting her to feel it all. She couldn't do that right now. Feeling it all would be too painful. A Dewar's on the rocks wouldn't.

Mariette eased onto a bar stool. Geoffrey Bulter sidled up on the next stool. "Good morning, Miss Stuart."

"Mr. Bulter, hello!"

"I overheard you calling Christian Stanislaus *Player.*"

"What? Oh, yes. I call him that from klavierspieler, short for piano player to the world."

"Oh, my dear, you are an innocent, aren't you? You don't know, do you? But, you've got it right, Miss Stuart. Christian Stanislaus is player to the world. On the circuit, he's notorious for that. His reputation is that he tickles as many ladies' bottoms as he does piano keys."

Mariette said, "That's not true."

"Think about it, Miss Stuart. How often do you see him? What does he do with the rest of the time when you are not there?"

"He's on tour. Plays his piano. Has recitals."

"Think about it, Miss Stuart." Geoffrey Bulter walked away.

Coming to her with a broad grin, the bartender said, "Sorry I took so long. It gets crazy when the fraternal organizations breakfast here. What can I get for you?"

"Nothing," Mariette said, rising from the stool. "Nothing at all."

Chapter 14

When Carlotta heard the kitchen door open, she said, "Where have you been? What's happened?" She turned from the sink, drying her hands. "Well, from the silly grin on your face, I think I know what happened. How was it?"

"Far surpassed all my expectations," she said, chuckling. One night with Player, and she was already sounding like him.

Carlotta looked around. "So where is he now?"

"Flying to Frankfurt."

"Will you see him again?"

"Of course. I could've gone with him—if I had a passport. I'll see him again in January when he plays San Diego."

"So, that's still on? San Diego, I mean."

"Of course."

"Want some company?"

"Well, sure, but I thought you wanted to stay here to be near Jerry the Florist."

Carlotta shook her head. "Nope. That's hopeless. Jerry the Florist is not interested in the game of love. Only the game of football with a few tight skirmishes during the time-outs. If I have to pretend I'm interested in the point spread one more time, I'll scream. Soon enough, you'll have the same problem with Christian and his music."

Mariette shook her head. "No, he doesn't force that on me. He wasn't even bothered that I missed his concert. But I am finding his music interests me on my own."

"Oh no." Carlotta gasped. "A true woman in love. She even finds the man's interests interesting."

Carlotta's words impressed Mariette. Was she in love? She wasn't sure. Everything always happened so rapidly with that man.

"But San Diego is still on, right?"

All Mariette knew was she'd never felt that way about Robert.

"Earth to Mariette! Earth to Mariette!"

Mariette broke into gales of laughter. "I am on planet Earth. Player checked our coordinates first thing this morning."

"Mariette! Do you still want me to go to San Diego with you or not?"

The question sobered her. "Of course, 'Lotta. You're my best friend. I still want to room with you if you want to come."

"I won't interfere with you and your piano player?" Carlotta pointed to Christian's photo on the bulletin board.

"Player's on the road until January 20. Then he comes to San Diego. If we have to, I'll stay in his hotel room."

"No, I'll stay in the hotel room. He can stay with you."

"You should have seen the room he had. It was a suite. Whirlpool bath. Wet bar. Phone by the tub."

"I get the picture. So you two aren't moving in together?"

"No, good heavens! That wasn't even discussed. Right now, I'm going to UC–San Diego, and he's on his concert tour."

"Whew! Well, that's good. Let's start packing and leave this town. La Jolla, here we come."

Chapter 15

Carlotta looked at her watch. It was 10:30 a.m. Mariette said Christian's plane got in at 10:00 a.m. So he would either be here in seconds—or if I-5 was backed up, it could take forever. No matter, she'd stall until he got here. Carlotta had to see the man who'd helped turn Mariette Stuart into a Pacific Ocean sea nymph.

As she put on her lipstick, the doorbell rang. She checked her hair in the downstairs mirror and waited until the doorbell rang again before she opened the door.

Standing before Carlotta was a tall, gorgeous Adonis. His face was beautifully chiseled with lines a sculptor could study for years in hopes of recreating a perfect male. She gasped when she saw him. "Oh my goodness! You're even better looking than your pictures."

His clear gray eyes looked her up and down. "Good heavens! So are you. And certainly more lifelike."

"You've never seen pictures of me."

"How do I know you've seen any of me? And this isn't the most sophisticated come-on I've ever heard."

Suddenly taken aback, Carlotta was indignant in her defense. "Because I'm Mariette's roommate. And she's got your pictures splattered all over the place."

Flashing the smile she'd seen on his album cover, Christian quietly said, "I know who you are, Carlotta. And it's a pleasure meeting you."

Carlotta reveled in the bowing of his head. It was so natural and flattering. "Now, that's a sophisticated come-on. Oh, you are smooth. And fun. You got any brothers?"

He held up two fingers. "One older, one younger."

"Any of them look like you?"

"My younger brother looks more like me than I do. Frank always says I'm the prototype and he's the finished product."

Looking Christian up and down one more time, Carlotta said. "Oh! Sounds good. Now cut to the chase."

Standing back, Christian tried to absorb the energetic little redhead with the rapid hand gestures. "Excuse me?"

"Is he connected?"

"Connected? Do you mean with organized crime? No, I don't believe so."

"No. Is he single, divorced, or—heaven forbid—married?"

Laughing, Christian shook his head. "Frank's a widower with a little boy named Corby."

Her effervescence popped, Carlotta sighed. "Hey, ho. I'm looking to be a lover not a substitute mommy."

Christian shrugged. "Hey, ho."

Mariette's voice reverberated down the stairs. "Carlotta! You were on your way out the door."

"I am, I am. I had to let the gentleman in first."

Mariette started down the staircase, casting a withering glance at Carlotta.

"I'm going. I'm going." Travel bag in hand, Carlotta headed for the door. She stopped and turned to Christian. "It was nice meeting you."

He bowed his head. "The pleasure was mine."

"I like him, 'Ette. He's a keeper," Carlotta said and slammed the door.

Left alone in blissful silence, Mariette and Christian devoured each other with their eyes.

"How was your flight?" Mariette felt mesmerized as she glided down to the landing. A shapely thigh pushed though her short kimono with each step she took. Padding toward him, she lifted her tresses up and away from her neck, releasing them as they tumbled back down.

"Fine. How is your new school?" Christian unfastened the button of his suit coat and moved beneath the light of the ceiling fan in the center of the vestibule.

"Fine. Take long to get here?" Facing him, Mariette's tongue slowly traced the contour of her lips, which had suddenly gone dry from the high-powered charge between them.

"No. No traffic." He watched her mouth glisten.

"Taxi or bus?" On the landing, her waist was encircled by his arm.

"I drove." He drew her nearer until she was in his shadow.

As she looked up, her raven hair went from the darkness of his shadow into the ceiling fan's light, iridescent as it passed into the bright rays.

"I didn't know you did." Her gaze traveled down to his mouth and coursed back up.

"What?" His hot breath on her cheeks made them flush.

"Drive." The rush of blood to her face started her panting.

"I do." He bent his head down to her.

"Oh." She gasped as his mouth surrounded hers. Once again, she was affected by a weakening in her knees, which was followed by a livening between her thighs.

"Where's you bedroom?" He swooped her in his arms.

"No. Put me down. I've dreamed of it here."

Sinking to his knees, Christian rested her on a sheepskin rug in the corner of the hallway. He untied her kimono. She was naked underneath. Maintaining control, he closed his eyes and turned away.

"No! Now, look at me."

Eyes not quite focused, he glanced at her and groaned.

"I have to undress you first. You just keep watching."

She could feel him tense and stiffen as she freed his broad shoulders from his suit coat. Unknotting his tie, she saw perspiration break out on his brow. He was trembling as she fumbled with his vest and shirt buttons. Suckling his thumb, she slipped the links through his french cuffs.

He groaned.

Her breasts skimmed his chest when she lifted the athletic T-shirt up and over his arms.

"Mariette. Please. Stop." His voice was guttural and raw.

Grabbing his chin in one hand, she undid his belt buckle and trousers with the other. "Don't talk," she said. "Feel."

Instructing him to stand, Mariette knelt before him and stripped the remaining clothes from him, freeing his maleness. "Oh," she cooed as she gazed at his pelvis. "Now, I've got to wrap this." She pulled a small square packet from her kimono pocket. Her teeth savagely ripped the foil holding the rubber sheath.

"I don't care if you paint it purple and tie it with ribbons," he growled. "Just hurry up. You're driving me insane."

Sheath in place, she pulled him down and climbed atop his pulsing hardness. "For all the times you've fantasized about this …" Bending forward, she rubbed her breasts on his chest. "It's finally come true." She sat up and started slowly rocking back and forth until he exploded with a primal, lascivious howl.

When he stopped thrashing, she rested spread-eagle atop him. She could feel his ferocious heartbeat answering hers. Next, she recalled, would come his enormous inhale of breath and a satisfied groan before his few moments of immobility set in. She started to slide off, but his hands quickly tightened around her biceps, holding her firmly on his chest. He confined her squirming legs with his powerful calves.

"No, you don't! You wicked woman. Enfeeble the prey and take off, eh?" He rolled over on top of her and captured her mouth.

She was pinned under his chest. He explored one ear with his tongue, and he stroked and pinched her other. Squirming under him in resistance, she could feel his hand snake down her side. Between her thighs it rested. His hand probed upward, and she started to shake as all her resistance floated away.

The rhythm of his fingers sent her soaring. Her crisis moved ever nearer. She was tottering on the edge of completion when he stopped. "No!" she cried as the tension he'd created was slipping. "More."

He sat up and calmly surveyed her, shaking his head. "Not alone you don't. This time, we make love together."

He replaced the sheath and entered her.

The ached-for pressure was finally within her. She moaned in expectation and want. His arm muscles flexed on either side of her, and he glared down in wanton lust as he moved in and out.

The fierceness in his eyes coupled with his powerful thrusts catapulted her over the edge in wave after wave of ecstasy. As her climax ebbed, she heard his soft cry.

They collapsed in a jumbled mass of arms and legs.

Still entangled, she clung to him. Finally, she said, "By the way, I haven't said hello. Hello."

He sat up, nestling her in his arms. "Mariette, I love you."

She trembled as he said it. There was gravity in his voice, focus in his eyes, and sincerity in his face. It was all so perfect. Then, a nagging little voice in the back of her head reminded her that so was the music he practiced over and over until it gave him the results he wanted. "I missed you," she said.

"Did you?"

"Oh, yes. We could've used a broad back when we were moving in here."

He smiled at her, rather sadly, she thought.

He shook his head. When he last left her, she was clinging to him at the airport and pleading with him to stay. And now she was back to her defensive tactic of teasing and not meeting his gaze. Would it always be like this? Each time he returned, would they be back to square one with her dodging and making light of her feelings?

He stared at that beautiful face that couldn't look him in the eye. However long it took, he'd wait it out until she was comfortable with whatever it was she felt.

"You still need a broad back—or are you pretty much settled?"

She felt quite content in his arms. "We're pretty much all moved in. What I need is help filling the larder. Carlotta says we need staples. I told her I have some in my desk drawer. She says they're the wrong kind. So, if you could go shopping with me, that would be great. Also, we can get whatever it is that you eat. I haven't been able to figure that out yet. It seems you have red meat and wine one day and boiled vegetables and brown rice the next. Not a lot of consistency there. Or are you on some kind of shock-the-body diet?"

"No." He laughed. "What I eat depends on whether I'm staying put or flying out. If I'm flying, I eat rice and vegetables to avoid jet lag. If I'm staying put, I clog my arteries with red meat because I want the energy and I like the taste. The wine is strictly for flavor and snob appeal."

She tugged at her kimono under his body. "Eloquently put, especially the clogging part. I like that. I'm going upstairs to get dressed. Then we can go shopping."

When she returned, he had replaced the dark blue suit with blue jeans and a white T-shirt. There was a box folded into one of the sleeves, which made him look like he'd just walked from the set of a 1950s teenage-rebellion flick. It flattered him and was perfect for the balmy Southern California winter.

Mariette opened the front door. A Mercedes-Benz was parked in her driveway. She turned to him. "Yours?"

He nodded.

"Not exactly Econo-Rent-a-Heap is it?"

"No, it's not. I bought it out by the airport."

"Are you flying it out with you when you leave?"

He shrugged. "I'll either sell it back, store it, or leave it here."

Mariette shook her head. "Don't leave it here. I don't want the responsibility."

"Okay. Want to drive it?"

"Oh, no. Not on your life. I want to see your expertise behind the wheel. Until a couple of hours ago, I didn't even know you drove."

"I do."

"So you've said. Now, get in the car and show me."

They arrived at the supermarket in one piece after Mariette reminded Christian only twice that they weren't on the Autobahn. Inside the supermarket, she watched as he filled the cart. Someone else could decide what a staple was. She was happy to tag along and let her mind wander.

She watched his back as he pinched tomatoes. What had he meant by *I love you*? It was so unexpected. He weighed out onions and tossed them in a sack. She knew some men said those words to gain a woman's favors, but he'd said them right after hers had been given. Garlic and shallots were chosen and bagged. Robert used to say those words to shut her up and leave him be, but she hadn't been nagging when Christian said them. He's brought it up on his own and out of the blue. She followed as he moved to lettuce and green things. Maybe he just wanted to be in love—and she was handy. *At least he hadn't pressed for affirmation in return.*

The overflowing basket finally registered in Mariette's mind when Christian ordered three filet mignon steaks from the butcher.

"Good heavens," she gasped. Garlic, anchovies, parsley, artichokes, asparagus, swiss chard, and unknown packages wrapped in white packed the cart on top of flour, sugar, cornmeal, olive oil, salt, and countless spice bottles. "Who's going to cook all of this?"

Careful not to squash the bread, he laid the latest package on top. "I am."

"Oh, really. Who taught you to cook?"

"My mother. Didn't yours teach you?"

"No. My mother taught me to marry a man who could afford to hire me a cook."

"Oh! My pleasure. Now, how many would you like?" He added a jar of cornichons to the heap. "I think three. One Italian. One French. One Chinese."

Mariette shook her head. This was the wrong man to use a smart comeback on. "Just get in line. I'm getting hungry."

As Christian loaded the foodstuffs onto the moving ramp, he turned back to Mariette. "Too provincial, eh? How about Creole and Thai chefs?"

"Christian!"

Finished unloading the cart, he beamed at her all wide-eyed and innocent. "Yes?"

She sputtered for words that would make him stop his nonsense. "Stuff it."

"Oh, I thought we'd have steak tonight. I'll stuff the veal breast tomorrow." He held up his hands in mock surrender. "I'll stop."

***

Back in her kitchen, Mariette puzzled out places for the larder while he cooked.

At the chopping block, Christian ran a French knife over a steel to create a burr in its edge. He grabbed an onion and halved it. Deftly, he sliced it two ways and madly chopped away. The knife came down ferociously fast.

Mariette winced at the rapid banging of carbon steel on wood. "Can I ask a stupid question?"

Christian looked up for a second and grabbed the other onion half. "Shoot."

Mariette kept her eyes glued on his rapid chopping. "What happens if you cut yourself?"

Christian froze, and his face blanched. His hands halted and went limp. His eyes went blank, and his mouth dropped open.

Mariette was shocked. Did the thought never occur to him? She imagined pictures going through his mind of severed or partially jointed fingers. Those beautiful hands truncated. His career ruined. Instantly, she regretted bringing it up. She reached out for him.

He said, "I bleed. Want to see?"

She couldn't believe his words. She was ready to haul off and hit him. But looking at his beautiful smile, she laughed until tears came to her eyes. "No, I don't want to see." Playfully, she slapped one of his biceps.

"Thank you for slapping rather than punching."

"Just be careful with that knife," Mariette said.

"It is a little dull. Got a sharpening stone?"

"Don't sharpen it. It will be worse if you cut yourself."

He began slicing potatoes. "*Au contraire,* my dear. It's easier to cut myself with a dull knife than a sharp one. Too much pressure needed to accomplish the task. Cut myself every time."

"Just don't talk about it, okay? It gives me the willies."

After slicing the potatoes, he put the knife away. Leaning across the counter, he took her hand. "Mariette, I can't live my life in fear that something's going to happen to my hands. It would make me neurotic and too careful. I'd strangle in that. And so would my music." He pulled up straight and shrugged.

He circled potatoes around the bottom of a frying pan, added olive oil, and put it on a burner.

He wrapped black peppercorns in a dish towel and crushed them with a rolling pin. His boyish smile was back. "You're afraid of discovering ice water in my veins?"

"Hardly. You're too passionate for that." She kissed him on the mouth as she passed by, looking for a place for the pickles. In a way, he was right. She knew he would bleed like normal people but damned little else.

He flamed the steak au poivre with cognac to her delight, and the Cabernet Sauvignon he'd selected was the best wine she'd ever tasted. The pears and Gorgonzola cheese with warm french bread for dessert made her feel decadent and overfed. She lifted her wineglass to him. "My compliments to the chef."

He bowed his head, refilled her glass, and said, "That advice of your mother's? Maybe you should eliminate the middleman and just marry the cook?"

"Very funny."

Christian looked at Mariette and into his wineglass. That was a little too subtle. Even he wouldn't have thought that comment serious. Standing, he asked, "Are you done?"

She nodded.

He came around, pulled out her chair, and took her hand.

"Where are we going?"

"To the sitting room for after-dinner port and cigars."

"I don't smoke."

"Neither do I."

He escorted Mariette to the sofa and paced the room. He walked over to the sliding glass doors, and his hunt ended at the windows. He immediately returned to Mariette. Sinking down before her on one knee, he fumbled the box from his shirtsleeve. He held the box before her eyes, and his thumb flipped the lid open. "Mariette, will you marry me?"

The largest, greenest emerald ring she had ever imagined appeared before her eyes. It was as big as a thumbnail in the shape of a teardrop with little diamonds huddled around in support. Mariette gasped at the man supplicating at her knee. His face was earnest and entreating. He held the tiny box in his hands as if it were his heart. Mariette's hands shot out to shield her from the sight. Her fingers closed, lowering the lid. "Put it away, Christian. Please. It makes me nervous." Her eyes burned as bright as the emerald she'd covered.

The box was rolled back into Christian's shirtsleeve. Hurt, confusion, and disappointment crossed his face. Finally, concern darkened his face and voice. "Mariette, do I make you nervous?"

His soft plaintive voice pulled her from herself. "Oh, no!" she said. "Well … some of the things you do, yes."

His hands gently encircled hers. "I don't mean to. Is it our intimacy? Does that make you nervous?"

She shook her head firmly. "No. That's the best part. No, wait! It's not the sex. It's talking with you. That's the best."

"Then what is it I do that makes you nervous? Can you give me an example? Please."

She wanted to answer him, but she didn't know how to put it into words. Being with him brought the exhilaration of summiting the highest peak in the world and the panic of finding its air too rare to breathe.

"Well, it's not just this, but ... where you had that ring stashed all day. That makes me nervous. All the way to the supermarket and back in your shirtsleeve!"

"Oh. I thought keeping it close would help build up my courage to propose."

"What if you lost it?"

"It's insured. I'd hardly try to entice you with an uninsured ring."

"Christian, a ring that big is not an enticement. It's outright bribery."

"All right." He laughed. "I'm bribing you if that's what you want to call it. If you don't like this ring, I'll get you another. It doesn't have to be an emerald. It doesn't have to be that size. I bought that one because I thought it matched your eyes, but you can have whatever you want."

"Player, I don't know what I want." The words slipped out before she knew it. She pulled back from him and instantly returned. "Yes. Yes, I do. I want some time. This is all very sudden. I just need some time."

What was sudden about it? He wouldn't have bedded her if his intentions weren't honorable. And that was months ago. He inhaled deeply to hold his composure. Well, for what it was worth, at least she was back to calling him Player. "All right, but I want you to tell me when I do things that make you nervous. Can you do that?"

"Why? Are you going to change them?"

He shrugged. "How could I say until I know what they are?"

Mariette playfully swatted at the box in Christian's sleeve. "Well, for starters, you can put that somewhere safe."

He bowed his head. "My pleasure. I will. And thank you for swatting rather than jabbing me."

Chapter 16

Like two children wary of the territory they'd broached, Mariette and Christian found solace, that night, sleeping in each other's arms. At daybreak, Mariette wakened, untangled herself from Christian, and put on her bathing suit. Confident his sleeping hours were still in confusion, Mariette went out to the patio and grabbed her wet suit for a quick scuba lesson. She'd be back before he woke up.

She watched him as he slept; he was pretty in repose. His brow didn't furrow. His mouth didn't gape in awful snorting. And best of all, he didn't twitch when he slept. Sleeping with him was not at all like sleeping with Robert. Mariette kissed him lightly on the cheek.

Christian murmured and rolled over.

Driving to the La Jolla branch of Scripps Canyon, Mariette's thoughts went to the night before. She'd slept with the question in her mind, and she hadn't risen with the answer. Why had he proposed? What did Christian really want? With Robert, she'd found out much too late that he was only interested in working his way up the corporate ladder. Being the boss's daughter, Mariette had been the perfect accessory for Robert—right up there with his Rolex and car phone. Mariette was an acquisition commensurate with Robert's lusted-after position in the business world.

That was the case with Christian. He was already well ensconced in his career. He didn't need any of her imagined influence with relatives, of which she had none in his line of work. And if he was looking for an accessory to complete his package, he would have proposed to someone similar to that ex-fiancée of his. And it certainly wasn't money he wanted from her. She had none, only the paltry inheritance from her father, which she and her mother shared. Christian appeared to have plenty of money of his own. If not, he was doing an incredible impression of a rich young man who couldn't spend it fast enough. That was something he did that made her nervous.

If it wasn't money or influence, what was it? Why did Christian want to marry her? Mariette pulled the Mustang onto Torrey Pines Road and turned off the radio.

Maybe it was a family thing. Maybe Christian was trying to recreate his parent's marriage. Robert had tried that. He'd even tried to perfect it to his own satisfaction. Robert had two mistresses in town, whereas his father kept only one. Mariette knew very little about Christian's parents. His father tuned pianos, and his mother taught Christian to cook. Maybe that was something she should ask about.

Mariette parked the Mustang.

A bright red Volvo pulled up and parked next to Mariette's car. Geoffrey Bulter approached and called out. "Well, good day, Miss Stuart." Smile plastered on his face, he eyed Mariette up and down.

"Mr. Bulter? Hello. Visiting La Jolla?" Mariette asked.

"No. Just transferred to the Music Department at UC–San Diego," Bulter said.

"Oh, congratulations."

"Still seeing Christian Stanislaus, I noticed. You know he sleeps around when he's on tour."

Is he stalking me? "Well, I've got a diving lesson. Have to go. Good luck at your new job, Mr. Bulter."

Mariette pulled on the wet suit before she got to the sand and she joined her class. It was the first time during her diving lessons that she understood immediately what was being taught. She didn't need to concentrate solely on moving and breathing properly. It was beginning to become second nature. After three more lessons, she'd be ready for certification.

On her return to her apartment, Mariette went straight to the back deck to hose off her wet suit. Christian was doing push-ups in her living room. She hung the suit to dry and went inside.

"So that's how you keep your biceps and chest muscles solid. I thought it was strictly from playing the piano."

"Seventy-three, seventy-four, seventy-five." Christian collapsed, held a few seconds, and rolled over. "No," he said between rapid breathing. "Playing is great for fingers and forearms, but it caves in the chest and is lousy for posture."

She crouched on all fours and crawled over to him. Close enough to kiss him, she shook her damp head, sprinkling salt water on him.

He grabbed her and pulled her on top of him. "Good morning, sea nymph."

Licking sweat and salt water from his temples, she replied, "Good morning, landlubber." She thought a second and smiled. "Do you skin-dive?"

"No."

"You should. There's a whole different world down there. Huge schools of fish. Immense coral forests. Kelp as big as trees. Today, I saw a clam digging his home into the side of a cliff. He dug in and disappeared, leaving nothing but a tiny hole. And he's not alone in there. That cliff is festering with them. It was marvelous."

Her smile was contagious, and he caught it. She'd taken a risk, and it was paying off. A brand-new world was hers. Her eyes sparkled when she spoke of it. He was delighted to see her like this.

"You're a strong swimmer," Mariette continued. "I can personally attest to that. And skin diving is easy. Best of all, it's underwater."

"I am not a particularly strong swimmer. I was just personally motivated that one time. And I did try skin diving once."

"Didn't you just love it?"

"I don't know, the pressure on my sinuses was too great. I couldn't stay under."

"Oh, pooh. A born landlubber."

"Oh, pooh? And just when you were beginning to think I was invincible."

A drop of moisture rolled down his cheek. She caught it with her tongue and traced its path back up to his temple. "That's okay. I like chinks in armor."

"That's good because I have more than you'd ever imagine. Speaking of which, would you mind if I got a piano and put it in this room?"

Mariette looked around her tiny living room. "Your Bösendorfer?"

Christian shook his head. "My Bösendorfer's nine and a half feet long. It would be a tad ostentatious in here, don't you think? No, I'm talking about a little spinet I could rent and stick in a corner. It really is necessary. If I don't have one handy, I get peculiar. It's one of my little chinks."

"Peculiar, huh? Foaming at the mouth and howling peculiar?"

"No. More like curling up in a ball and whimpering peculiar."

"That sounds more like a big chink."

He nodded. "Especially when I start trying to chew my hands off."

"Oh, yuck! All right. You can have a piano." She pointed to the windows. "Over there will be fine." She shivered at the thought. "I don't want to see anyone suffer piano withdrawal."

"Bless, you. You'll be very glad you did." He walked over to the windows. "Perfect. I love a view."

Mariette took Christian to the mall and found a store that rented, sold, and leased pianos, organs, and keyboards.

Christian removed his arm from Mariette's shoulder and went directly to the salesman. He told the man he wanted to rent a spinet, gave the address where it was to be delivered and the credit card it was to be charged on, and proceeded to try out various instruments.

As Christian played a variety of diverse movements on the fourth piano, the salesman turned to Mariette and said, "He's good."

"Do you really think so? He has delusions of someday doing it for a living." She shook her head and whispered, "I try to discourage it. No use getting his hopes up."

"No," the salesman protested. "You shouldn't. He's very good."

"Yes, but who'd hire him to play that stuff?"

"Heavens. I would—for one. He'd draw people. Increase sales."

"Well, that's a very nice thing to say." Mariette patted the man's hand as Christian moved to a fifth spinet. "Perhaps you could tell him that. Make him feel his practicing isn't for naught. Maybe he could do something during the day. He's busy nights." She nodded to the man confidentially. "Janitor for the school district, you know."

Christian joined them at the sales desk. He pointed to a cherrywood spinet. "That one will be fine."

The salesman finished filling in the papers he'd drawn up and turned them over for Christian to sign. "Sir, if you ever tire of sweeping out classrooms and are interested in a day job, I'd love to offer you one."

Christian turned around to see if there was someone behind him and turned back to the salesman. "I beg you pardon."

"Yes, I'd pay you to do what you've just done here."

"Check the voice on different pianos?" Christian shot Mariette a suspicious look. What had she precipitated?

"Yes. Play whatever you wish. On any of the instruments."

Christian signed his name to complete the transaction. "Thank you, sir. I'll keep it in mind." He grabbed Mariette and headed for the door.

The salesman called after them, "It would definitely be more fulfilling than sweeping floors."

Christian looked back and nodded. "Yes, I'm sure that's true."

Outside the showroom, Mariette convulsed in laughter.

Incredulous, Christian turned to her. "What did you tell that man?"

"Not much. Just that you were a janitor for the school district who had a penchant for playing the piano and fancied himself rather good at it."

"Oh, is that all?"

She nodded and shot him an impish grin. "You are so much fun to watch when you're confused."

Taking her by the arm, Christian escorted her out of the mall. "I better get you back home. If you cause any more confusion, I won't be able to contain my lascivious urges."

Walking her back to the car, he muttered, "A penchant for playing. Unbelievable."

Motoring the Mustang down La Jolla Village Drive, Mariette was instructed to pull into a bank near her home. The parking lot was crowded, so she told Christian she'd circle the block until his business was through.

He shook his head. Holding up the engagement ring box, he said, "I'm getting a safety-deposit box for this. I want your signature on the card so you'll have access to it."

"Why? So, I can get it out someday, put it on, and wire you that we're engaged?"

"Wow! There's an idea."

"Wow, yourself. You're in luck. That car right there is pulling out."

***

After dinner, Mariette built a fire while Christian warmed the cognac. He pulled in the sheepskin rug from the entranceway and laid it in front of the hearth. The newspaper strips under the kindling were set ablaze, and she joined him on the rug. Handing her a snifter of cognac with one hand, he wiped a smudge of soot off her cheek with the other.

She liked how they mindlessly switched typically male-female roles with no forethought or fuss.

She lifted the glass to him. "Here's to you."

He touched his glass to hers. "*Nazdrowie!*"

She watched him over the snifter as she drank. "Is that toast Ukrainian or Polish?"

Eye contact with her was easy. He found it encouraging and fun. Maybe they should elope. Las Vegas was nearby; Tijuana was even nearer. They could hop in his heap and be there in an hour. "Both. They're both Slavic languages. Just different branches."

She saw a spark start in his eyes. "Did you speak both at home? Growing up. I mean."

He watched her watching him. That cute, determined little face had business on her mind. It was not the time to be impetuous. Caprice was not needed; patience was. He took a deep breath, exhaling slowly to attain composure. He was well versed in patience. Like learning a complex piece of music, he'd be precise and persistent until he worked it through. "At home, we spoke Ukrainian to my mother and English to my father."

She saw the spark in his eyes dissolve into detached curiosity. That was the third time she'd seen him do that. Once it happened in San Francisco, outside her hotel room. Another time, he'd done it in Cincinnati inside his hotel room. Now, it was happening again. One minute he was vibrant and in attendance with her, and the next minute, he was dispassionate, adopting an almost clinical pose. It brought back the chilling reminder of doctors at nursing school who coldly analyzed the most heartrending human conditions and summing them up as "interesting."

"Why speak one language to one parent and something different to the other?" she asked.

He looked into her green eyes and became lost in their confine, but she wasn't some Brahms symphony or Chopin étude. She was a beautifully complex woman who he could enamor one minute and estrange the next. He had no bearing with her. He felt like he was flying blind with no point of reference. Damn, the woman disarmed him. "My mother doesn't like to forget the past, so she keeps her language there. My father always looks to the future. His future is in America, so he speaks as Americans do."

She watched his aloofness falter, replaced by an endearing look of confusion. "How did they meet? Your parents."

"On a ship, coming to America."

She took hold of his hand. "Sounds romantic."

"I don't think so. Those ships were wall-to-wall people. There was no place to sleep. They sat on their belongings to keep them safe. Survived on whatever food and water they'd brought. My mother was trying to jump ship in the middle of the Atlantic when my father saw her. He ran over and pulled her from the railing."

"Oh, my! Why would your mother want to jump ship? That sounds so desperate."

It was not something Christian particularly cared to talk about. "Despondent, actually. She was the only one left in her family. Her parents had just been killed in a purge. She and her brother were fleeing the country when he was shot to death at the border. Apparently, it had been her brother's dream to come to America. Not hers. I guess she felt guilty about surviving. As if she had no right to be alive."

"And your father kept her from jumping?"

Hating the pall that story put on conversations, he tried to relate the rest with as much lightness as possible. "He dissuaded her by saying if she went in, he'd have to go in after her—and he didn't know how to swim."

A fleeting smile passed Mariette's face. She meant no disrespect, but something about the reasoning in that story sounded so right and appropriate as a prelude to Christian's origins. "And that convinced her?"

Christian shrugged. "Well, it got her attention. He told her that being alive was a reason to celebrate and not a reason to feel guilty. Then he started telling her how wonderful America was. How people were joyous because they didn't have to expend all their energies just to keep from perishing. How the government didn't shoot people because of what they said or thought or because they wanted the people's land or food. He expected his life to be wonderful but for one thing: he needed someone by his side. So, he proposed to her."

"And?"

"And my mother accepted. They got married on the ship."

"And lived happily ever after."

He leaned forward and pecked her on the mouth. "Liebchen, it's not a fairy tale. It's just life. They have their problems like everyone else. They just prefer to be together and share them."

"Well, does your father know how to swim?"

"Like a fish."

She started to laugh. "Did he at the time?"

"Oh, yes."

She nodded. So he came from a family of men who instilled reasons for living in the lives of women they'd saved from mortal danger. She liked that Christian had done for her what his father had done for his mother.

Touching his hand, Mariette puzzled over the next question. How could she tactfully ask Christian if his father kept a mistress? It was a vulgar question and none of her damned business, but it was something that was gnawing at her and wouldn't go away. From what she'd been told, Christian followed very closely in his father's footsteps. It would be helpful to know if his father kept a mistress.

"I don't know," Christian said.

Mariette stared at him. "You don't know what?"

"Whether or not my father has a mistress."

"I didn't ask that."

"Well, no. You wouldn't. It's just good manners not to. But I would think after being married to a man whose father kept a mistress, thereby prompting the son to take one, it might be something you'd wonder."

"Two."

"Excuse me?"

"Two, Robert had two mistresses."

"Simultaneously?"

Mariette nodded.

"Two. Really? And a wife?" Christian shook his head in amazement. "Energetic sort, isn't he?"

"Greedy sort is more like it." Mariette threw that diversion into the conversation in case Christian needed an easy escape from the odious topic. She waited to see if he'd take it or plow on.

"Offhand, I'd say no. My father has no mistress. He's very devoted to my mother. I do believe if she had gone overboard, he would have gone in after her, but in truth, I don't know. I do know if I asked him, he'd tell me to mind my own business. What I don't know is if he'd tell me that before or after he knocked my block off for being such a wisenheimer."

Mariette took both of Christian's hands and wrapped his arms around her. She entwined her arms under his and squeezed his rib cage. It was strange how her thoughts were so transparent when she was with him.

Seductively, he kissed her while pushing her back on the sheepskin rug.

"Mm," Mariette muttered. "I knew there was something I was going to love about this rug when I bought it."

***

The next morning, Christian's travel alarm went off at six. He grabbed it—bent on throwing it across the room—and stopped and smiled. He recognized the room; he knew where he was. Beside him, Mariette slept curled up like a kitten. It was wonderful waking up with her at his side. He wanted it to be like that for the rest of their lives. Now, he just had to convince her of it. Kissing her temple, he slipped from the bed.

At the washroom basin, he set out his razor, shaving brush, mug, a bottle of solution to soften his beard, and a bottle of solution to anoint his skin after he scraped it clean. He had just started lathering his shaving brush when Mariette came in. She brought in a chair and sat beside the basin. Smiling, he touched her nose with his shaving brush. She immediately wiped off the lather.

"I'm not here to fool around," she said. "This is serious." Her somber face reinforced her statement.

"Of course." He held up the shaving brush to his chin. "Can I continue what I'm doing?"

"Of course." She watched his eyes go to the mirror as he lathered his face. "You said I should tell you when you do things that make me nervous."

He put the brush back in the shaving mug and picked up his razor. "Yes, I did."

"One of the things that bothers me most—"

Lifting his chin, he stretched the skin on his neck. "Only one?"

"Do you want to hear this?"

"I'm all ears."

"What you did with the ring yesterday?"

"I put it in a safety-deposit box."

"Yes. Then you made me an alternate signer on the card and gave me a key."

Carefully, he maneuvered the blade around his Adam's apple. Finishing with his neck, he looked over to Mariette. "That's so you can have access to it if and when you want."

"Suppose I take the ring and hock it?"

He regarded his razor. It wasn't doing a very good job. He twisted the handle's bottom to open the blade's housing and replaced it. "You could. But hocking it won't get you much money. If that's what you're interested in, you'd be better off asking me for however much money you want."

"And you'd give it to me?"

New razors always nicked him. He never adjusted the pressure of his hand quickly enough for the deft touch they required. Carefully, he commenced shaving. "Sure."

"That's what I'm talking about."

"What?"

Her eyes followed his movements as she spoke. "Your attitude toward money. You're like kid in a candy store with a twenty-dollar bill. A generous kid, I'll grant you, but still a kid buying everything in sight."

His head held still, he glanced down to her and looked back to the mirror. "I try to do my share to keep the economy afloat."

"It's not expected you do it single-handedly. How much money do you make a year?"

"I don't know." All too often, he clipped himself under his right cheekbone. He slowly passed through the area. "Enough."

"How much is that? Roughly?"

The razor set down, Christian turned to her. "Mariette, I make an indecent amount of money for something I absolutely love doing." He grabbed the shaving brush again. "Admittedly, I don't handle the money well."

"What's an indecent amount? Six figures?"

He figured in his head how many zeroes six figures. "About."

"You gross one hundred thousand dollars a year!"

"No. It's more like three hundred thousand, what with concertizing, CD sales, and public appearances. I think I net about two hundred thousand—maybe less."

"Holy smoke! And what do you do with it?"

He picked up the razor and spoke slowly as he shaved his left cheek. "Well, I used to keep it under the mattress, but I move around too much and it got too …" He caught the impatient look on her face in the mirror's reflection and stopped. "I have a financial manager."

She nodded her approval. "What does he have you invested in?"

"My dear, that's his job. That's what I pay him for. He doesn't tell me how to play sonatas. And I don't tell him what the best investments are."

"My sweet man, if you don't know what your financial manager is doing with your money, you are a fool. And you know what happens to a fool and his money? They are soon parted."

"Ow!" He knew he'd nick himself. "Well, this fool and his money were damned lucky to get together to begin with."

She didn't want to laugh at his words. She was speaking about something very serious. Her father would turn over in his grave if he heard Christian gave his financial manager free rein. But he was making her chuckle anyway.

Christian regarded Mariette as he moistened the styptic pencil. "So what does the banker's daughter recommend the fool do?"

She was pleased he remembered her father. "The banker's daughter suggests you have a diverse portfolio. Some real estate. Some stocks. Of course mutual funds. Maybe even some futures. But most of all, you need a financial analyst you trust implicitly."

He touched the styptic pencil to his cut. "Are you applying for the job?"

"Oh, no! I'm just making some intelligent suggestions. I don't want to be saddled with the future of your money."

Christian bent down to the washbasin and rinsed the remaining lather from his face. "Okay."

"Do you happen to have your financial statement with you?"

"No."

Mariette grabbed his bottle of bay rum, opened it, and took a whiff. It smelled better when it was mixed with his masculine scent. "Could you get a copy?"

He took the proffered bottle. "Sure."

"I just want to take a look."

"Fine."

"Really, that's all."

"I believe you. You're the one having doubts."

She took the bay rum back, sniffing it again. Before she recapped the bottle, she dabbed a bit on her index finger and touched behind each ear lobe. Now that she thought about it, seeing how much disposable income he could afford to play with might be fun. There was high-tech stock in growth companies. Gold. Foreign currencies. And the United European Market was assembling soon. Trade embargoes were being dropped with the East. Walls were coming down in Eastern Europe. Yes, the banker's daughter could have some fun.

As he washed his hands, she tossed a towel over his shoulder. "I just want to make sure your backside is covered."

"Thank you."

"Shower next?"

"Yes, but, alas, I must do it alone. You're too much of a distraction."

Chapter 17

Carlotta and Mariette were meeting at their favorite greasy spoon for breakfast. As usual, Carlotta was half an hour late. Mariette wasn't there at all. Grabbing the booth she wanted, Carlotta sat back and pondered. 'Ette was never late for anything. In fact she was usually fifteen minutes early. Carlotta sighed and grabbed the menu she knew by heart. Things were moving awfully fast for her best friend. Carlotta knew that wasn't really Mariette's style. 'Ette liked to go slowly and mull things over again and again. Think them to death. Then just when Carlotta was ready to give up on Mariette making any sort of decision at all, Mariette would accomplish things at lightning speed.

Carlotta had been sure after Mariette's breakneck pace of dumping Robert and going back to school that she'd settle down to a quiet nursing career. Instead, Mariette ditched nursing and moved out to California. Now, she was taking scuba lessons, priming for a career in marine biology, and going out with this incredible hunk of a man while Carlotta was still trying to catch her breath. Oh well, Carlotta would catch up and take back the lead. She always had.

Carlotta twisted around to look at the clock behind the counter. She could just make out the hands through the grease and lint. It looked like ten thirty. So, where was 'Ette? She shook her head. *That's what happens when your best friend meets someone special. You're expected to step aside and wait.* Heaven knows that Carlotta would expect the same.

Mariette's blue Mustang screeched into the parking lot. After slamming and locking the car door on her sweater twice, Mariette finally made it through the entrance of Biggies Burger and Grill.

Carlotta watched Mariette's tan little body slide into the bench seat opposite her. Mariette didn't look so hot. Her mouth was set in a thin-lipped frown, and there was a nasty wrinkle between her eyebrows where she crunched them together.

"Are you okay, 'Ette?"

Menu raised to her face, Mariette nodded. "Yeah, I'm okay."

"You don't look okay."

"I said I'm all right." Her voice cracked as she spoke.

"What's wrong? What'd he do?"

Letting out an exasperated sound, Mariette shook her head. "No, it's me. He hasn't done anything." She shrugged and sniffed back tears. "Well, yeah. He proposed."

"He proposed? Congratulations!" Carlotta squealed and composed herself. "No, excuse me. It's 'best wishes' to the bride and 'congratulations' to the groom."

"I didn't say I accepted."

Carlotta was at a loss. When she'd left at the beginning of the week, Mariette was running around the apartment, singing and barely able to contain herself while waiting for her piano player to arrive. Now, Mariette looked like she hadn't slept for three days.

"Well, that's good 'cause you look miserable." Carlotta grabbed the menu from Mariette and put it back between the napkin dispenser and sugar holder. "Come on, 'Ette. Tell me what happened."

"I don't know. Nothing." She picked up the menu again and opened it. Dropping the menu in front of her, she looked up at Carlotta. "Something's wrong. There's this fellow, Geoffrey Bulter. He was my music appreciation teacher in Cincinnati last year. When Christian flew out of the airport, Mr. Bulter overheard me calling Christian Player. Christian's plane left, and Bulter tracked me down and told me that Christian is a player. He's known on the circuit for fooling around. Bulter said he tickles as many women's bottoms as he does piano keys."

"How would he know Christian?"

"They played off each other in some piano competition ten years ago, and Christian won. Well, I didn't believe Bulter. I thought it was piano competition jealousy, so I ignored it. Well, yesterday before my scuba lesson, Geoffrey Bulter parks next to my car. He said he transferred to the UC–San Diego music department. He told me he knew I was seeing Christian and reminded me what he had said and asked if I really trusted Christian away on tour. Just now, I saw Bulter's car circling the parking lot."

"That's creepy. Have you told Christian about this?"

"Not yet. I think it's strange, Bulter transferred from the University of Cincinnati music department to the UC–San Diego music department. It freaks me. I can't figure it. Is Bulter stalking me? Is he stalking Christian?"

"You'd better talk to Christian."

Chapter 18

After their intimacies, Mariette rolled over in her bed and said, "Christian, you are a very amorous man."

"Thank you, Mariette. I guess. What's all this about?"

"What do you mean?"

"What are you getting at? Something's on your mind. What?"

"What do you do on the road?"

"On the road?"

"You know, when you're away for weeks or months at a time."

"When I'm away on tour, I practice—endless hours of practicing, playing thousands of notes from memory. Keeping current with my itinerary. I travel from one hall to another, concertizing with the realization that no matter how well I do, I will never give the perfect performance—but I keep trying. Why are you asking?"

"I just wondered what an amorous, passionate man like you does with all that passion when he's away on tour."

Christian sat up, leaned against the headboard, and looked down to Mariette. "I sublimate the passion into my music."

"Sublimate?"

"Yes, sublimate. Transform lascivious urges into socially acceptable activities. In my case, it's my music."

Mariette chuckled. "Are you inferring our lovemaking is lascivious?"

"I certainly hope so." He bent down and kissed her. "I much more look forward to channeling my lascivious urges through you than Mussorgsky or Barber or Chopin."

"I hope Mussorgsky, Barber, and Chopin are composers."

"They are." Christian walked over to the window and opened it. He turned back and said, "Look, Mariette, once we get married, I can take you with me. We'll travel, and you can see what I do. I want to warn you, though, that you'll probably be very, very bored most of the time because I practice, memorize, and concertize all the time."

His words did not assuage Mariette. She still remembered Robert's excuses for being late, excuses for being intractable, and excuses for her messages not getting through to him.

Christian sat back down on the bed and took her hand. "Mariette, I am not your ex-husband. I don't spread my seed all over whatever continent I'm on. That drains vital energy and is very bad for creativity. If you don't believe me, ask Klaus. My manager always knows where I am and what I'm doing."

"Except when you got *wayward* and took me on the cable car to Fisherman's Wharf. How often do you get *wayward*, Christian?"

He scowled. "That one time. And I've been hearing about it ever since. Klaus does like to know where his cash cows are. Mariette, why are you so convinced that I sleep around?"

"I've heard that you have a girl in every port."

Rising from the bed, Christian pulled on his jeans. At the bedroom door, he turned around. His face was dark and contorted. His words were spat out coldly, "Look, Mariette, I don't sleep around when I'm on tour. Maybe Robert did that to you, but I don't."

Christian bounded down the stairs. In the living room, he glared at the spinet. He sat down and buried himself in Chopin's "Revolutionary Étude."

Mariette stayed in bed as the music seeped through the bedroom floor. The piece started out stirring and bold, but the music gradually became angry. Mariette tossed and turned, trying for sleep. When she finally drifted off, the music was simple and beautifully melodic. It abruptly switched to sounding like a cat being strangled.

Her sleep that night was fitful, and she woke to music so piercing and tender that it made her cry. She rolled over, letting the soft, touching music fill her dreams.

***

In the morning, Mariette woke with a start. She was still in bed, and the house was silent. In a panic, she rushed to the window and released the shade. Frantic, she surveyed the grounds. His car was in the driveway. Forehead pressed to the cool pane, she waited for her heart to calm. He was still around somewhere. But where? All she knew was that he hadn't come to bed. She threw on a kimono and slipped down the stairs.

The kitchen was empty. No steamed chocolate or french-roasted coffee were in the works this morning. Funny how quickly she'd come to rely on that. She went to the stove and felt the café filter contraption he'd bought. It was stone cold. So where was he?

She went into the hallway and rubbed her feet across the sheepskin rug to warm them. Maybe he'd never left the living room. He could've easily gotten tired, crawled over, and collapsed on the couch. She went to the door and listened. All was quiet. Turning the knob, she heard the bolt release with a pop. She waited. No sounds came from within. She pushed on the handle. The door opened slowly. Staying at the threshold, Mariette peered in.

Framed by the picture window, Christian was seated at the piano. He was slumped over with his head cradled in his arms on the keyboard.

Gingerly, Mariette walked over to his collapsed form. He was deep in sleep. Her immediate urge was to stroke his forehead with its jagged brow, but she stopped herself. They'd disturbed each other enough the previous night. Sleep was for the best. Quietly, she left the room.

In the kitchen, Mariette puzzled over the coffeemaker. She remembered it worked backward from the way she'd anticipated. In her mind, the water and ground coffee went in the wrong places.

The ringing of the phone saved her predicament. As she picked up the receiver, the answer became obvious. It was easier to go back to instant coffee and cocoa. Player could deal with the complicated way of doing things.

"Hello?"

"Miss Mariette Stuart, please."

"This is Mariette."

"Oh, Mariette. Hello. This is Grete Steiner."

"Grete! How good to hear from you. How are you?"

"I'm well. And you?"

"Fine. We're doing just fine."

"Oh, I'm glad to hear that. I'd love to chat, but let me get my business out of the way first. Then we talk. May I speak with Krischan?"

She really didn't want to wake him. "He's sleeping on his piano right now. He's been up all night playing. I don't think he's slept much and—"

"In one of his black moods, is he?"

"Black mood?" That didn't sound good. She thought of the darkness on his face when Christian swept from the room. "Is he dangerous when this happens? Does he get violent?" Mariette recalled arguments when Robert suddenly flared, lashed out, and—one time—struck her. Mariette threw Robert out of the house and divorced him after that.

"Krischan? Dangerous?" Grete's breathy laugh punctuated his name. "Hardly. As the artists go, he's one of our more benign ones." Grete's chuckling abruptly stopped. Concern filled the bubbly voice. "Mariette, why would you ask that?"

"Well, it got a little tense between us last night. He stormed out of the bedroom. And now I'm thinking about that woman he was engaged to. You know, the opera singer."

"Lucia LaTempesta. Yes, I know." Grete's voice turned very concerned. "What did he tell you about her?"

"That it was very ugly between them. Things were thrown. She threatened to smash his hands after he choked her. The two of them being pulled apart physically."

"Oh," Grete replied quietly. "Is that the story he tells about the accident? Figures he'd take the blame."

"What accident? What happened?" The other end of the line was silent. "Grete, please tell me what happened?"

"Krischan should be telling you this. Not me."

"I agree, but I've told you what he said and there was nothing about an accident."

Grete sighed deeply. She was mostly annoyed with herself for mentioning the accident, but she was also peeved that Christian had left so many loose ends dangling. "Well, seeing as he's being so bloody noble and tight-lipped about it, I'll tell you. But you'd better get the facts straight from Krischan because I wasn't there."

"Yes. Yes, I will. Please tell me."

"It was a long time ago. I was still in school. I remember waking up and my parents being in an incredible uproar. Mama screamed at my father that he should stay out of his clients' personal lives. He was lucky one hadn't seriously impaired the other."

"Grete, please. Go on."

"I don't know what brought this about. Krischan and Lucia were in my father's office. Lucia attacked Krischan with a straight razor, apparently aiming for his eye. Luckily, she caught him above it. Gouged through the skin to the bone. You may have noticed one of his eyebrows doesn't match the other. It was sliced clean through. I believe Senor Ernesto stopped the bleeding and sutured it closed with no help of a doctor. That's why it looks a little ragged. They couldn't risk any press on that sort of thing. So, everything was done very hastily.

"My father still feels miserable about the whole incident. It was poor judgment and bad business. It was unfair to both clients to force two temperamental artists together. He could have gotten one of them killed. My father's much better about interference now. Or he tries to be. He still views all the artists as his children though. At times, he becomes overly anxious regarding Krischan's personal life, which you've probably noticed from his inconsistency with you. A part of him wants to discourage Krischan from any delicate dealings with others. The sensible part realizes he'd only destroy what he's trying to protect."

"What did Player—I mean Christian—do? I hope he did choke her."

"Mariette, I don't know. I wasn't there. What I'm telling you is all secondhand and probably very distorted. This is something you should ask of Krischan."

"Yes. Of course, I will."

"Now, Mariette. I must get off the telephone. A crucial appointment has just arrived early. Why don't you have Krischan call me when he gets up? There's a change in his itinerary he needs to know."

"Certainly, I will. And, thank you, Grete."

"*Es ist schon gut. Und* Mariette? Don't worry about Krischan. I don't find him the least bit dangerous."

Mariette placed the telephone receiver back in its cradle. *Why in the world wouldn't Player tell me about the accident?*

Chapter 19

Christian Stanislaus woke up on the spinet. Not having done that in a good dozen years, his body reminded him why he'd dropped the nasty little habit. Stretching his neck muscles helped relieve the pain at the base of his skull. The killer stiffness between his shoulder blades was not so cooperative. He tried a few push-ups, but they were no help. At thirty-six, he was too old to be pulling such stupid tricks. So why the deuce had he played himself out until he collapsed? It must have had something to do with Mariette. She was the only one who could cause that deep a rooting through his soul nowadays.

Christian looked around the room. How long had he been at this? Was it the same day or the next? Glancing for his watch, he noticed all he had on was a pair of jeans. No wonder he was freezing. He went out to the hallway and looked around. No lights were on. Walking to the kitchen brought back their last conversation. So Mariette Stuart thought he cheated on her. Well, now she could add what a moody bastard he could be. He considered that a more accurate picture of himself.

There was a note in the kitchen from Mariette. "Off to class. Be back around 2 p.m. Love, Mariette."

Well, Christian thought, *she may think I'm a cheating bastard, but she signs: Love, Mariette. Odd that she can write it in a note but can't say it to my face.*

Christian telephoned his manager. "Klaus, can I speak with you?"

"Krystia Stanislaus wants to talk with his manager, and it isn't even a Wednesday? Quite the occasion."

"I'm serious. I've got something I want to tell you, and I'd like to do it in person. Do you have time?"

"Of course I have time. That's my job. You stay put. I'll come to you."

Christian looked around the room and shook his head. "You know where I am?"

"*Ja,* of course I know where you are."

Christian shivered. "You know, Klaus, it's kind of creepy that you always know where to find me."

"In case you haven't noticed for the past twenty years, I'm your manager. That's my job. See you in about an hour."

***

Klaus Steiner exited his mobile office, walked up the path, and entered Mariette's apartment. Christian was playing the piano. "Ah! 'Rach 2.' It sounds good. I could hear it all the way up the driveway. Keep it up. It's going well."

"*Danke,* Klaus."

Klaus looked around at the spindly chairs in the living room and plopped down on the sofa. "So, I'm here. Talk."

"The woman I've been seeing? Mariette Stuart?"

"*Ja.* I know. You've been seeing—and sleeping—with her?"

"I asked her to marry me."

"*Gut,*" Klaus replied.

"Good? You think it's good?"

"I just said so. *Ja?*"

"Well, after the Lucia fiasco, I wasn't sure what you'd think."

"The Lucia LaTempesta fiasco was ten years ago. Ancient history. You've matured a lot since then. So, offhand, my only suggestion to you is switch to an electric razor."

Christian brushed his left eyebrow. "You're not funny."

"Yes, I am. I'm hilarious." Klaus chortled. "Look, Krystia, my dear departed Alma had me and Ernesto swear we would never interfere again."

"Interfere with what?"

"Your selection of a wife."

"Alma said that?"

"*Ja.* She said, 'Krystia has to make his own choice of a wife—not what you and Ernesto decide who would be good for him.' *Und,* she said, 'Krystia should marry.'"

"Alma said that?"

"*Ja.* In case you hadn't noticed, which I'm sure you didn't, she was quite fond of you."

"You're right. I never noticed."

"Krystia, you are in your own mind so much that I'm surprised you're even aware of Fraulein Stuart."

"Isn't that what you and Maestro Lochner taught me when I was barely twelve: respect the gift that I was given and always keep my mind on the music?"

"And my uncle and I are very proud. You learned well to transmute your sexual energy into your music. And you have become a fine musician."

Klaus pulled a package of walnuts from his jacket pocket and offered one to Christian. "Walnut? Great brain food."

"*Nein, danke.*" Christian waved away the walnuts. "Let me understand what you're telling me. I've learned the transmutation technique so well that it's acceptable for me to have a wife now? Isn't that *counterproductive*?"

"*Nein.* The love and support of a good woman is essential for success. It frees your mind from having to even think about where your next intimacies are, and you can focus completely on your music." Klaus tossed a walnut into his mouth.

"When I'm not focusing on Mariette, of course."

"That's part of the package. Once you're married, things settle down."

"I don't know about things settling down, but I'll take your word for it."

"You said you proposed. Did she accept?"

"Not yet."

"So, what's the problem?"

"She was told that I sleep around when I'm on tour."

"Of course you sleep around. Depending on your schedule, you sleep in one hotel for a couple of nights before you go on to the next concert hall and hotel. Of course you sleep. You have to sleep."

"No, no. 'Sleeping around' is English slang for being sexually promiscuous."

"Sexually promiscuous, you? This Fraulein doesn't sound like she knows you very well at all. Are you sure you want to marry her?"

"Yes, I love her and want to marry her."

"Who told her that you are sexually promiscuous?"

"I'm not sure. I was on the spinet all night, playing and trying to figure it out. I finally passed out."

"*Zut, Krystia,* not that 'black mood' thing again? You did that when you were a kid. You'd stay at your piano and play until you collapsed. You're too old for that."

"Tell me about it. My back is killing me."

Klaus sighed. "Well, don't worry about this 'promiscuous' nonsense. I'll get to the bottom of that. Take a nice warm bath with Epsom salts and get back to 'Rach 2.' It's a big piece of music. It takes a long time—sometimes years—learning well."

"*Danke,* Klaus. I will. *Auf Wiedersehen.*"

***

Mariette answered the phone in her apartment. "Hello."

"*Fraulein Stuart, das est Klaus Steiner.*"

Flustered, Mariette answered, "Herr Steiner, oh! Hello. Christian isn't here."

"*Ja,* I know. He's in Toronto today. Plays with TSO tonight. He'll be back tomorrow. I wanted to speak with you—privately—not over the phone. Are you available?"

"Well, yes. I guess."

"*Gut.* I'll pull up in my office on wheels, *und* we meet in there."

***

Klaus Steiner opened his mobile office door. "*Ah, Fraulein Stuart.* We've spoken over the phone, *und* I wanted to meet you in person." He offers his hand. "*Ich heisse Klaus Steiner.* How do you do?"

Mariette replied, "And I'm Mariette Stuart. How do you do? This is very kind of you to meet me like this."

"Please come in."

Mariette entered Klaus's office on wheels. She glanced around. Desks, chairs, telephones, televisions, screens, and printers quietly whirred away or sat on standby.

"Who's slandering Krystia?"

"Excuse me?"

"Krystia Stanislaus has an incredible gift and reverence for his music, and he does not waste it. He was taught very early, even before puberty, to honor the gift, and he would never, ever disrespect that."

Mariette looked around. "Well, I don't know quite what you are saying. We do sleep together when he's in town. Is that what you're talking about?"

"*Ja.* I know you two sleep together. You're his first one."

"What?"

"You're the first woman Krystia has slept with."

Mariette shook her head. "That's not possible."

"*Ja,* it is."

"Christian? But he's so knowledgeable and sophisticated. And you're saying I'm his first?"

"*Nein,* technically, you're his second. His music is his first love and always will be, but you're the second."

"Wait a minute. I'm the first woman Christian Stanislaus has ever slept with? But he's so talented."

"*Ja,* he is. I can't believe how quickly he can pick up and play a composition he's never seen before either, but he can. He's a very talented man."

"Wait a minute, if I'm his first, what about the opera singer? Lucia? Didn't he go to bed with her?"

"Lucia LaTempesta?" Klaus shook his head. "*Nein.* That was never consummated. They were never married. They hated each other. That was a very bad move on mine and Ernesto's part."

"Christian was a virgin when we first went to bed? If I knew that, I don't know if I would have gone to bed with him."

Klaus shrugged. "Why not? He's got to start someplace. Seems to me it makes sense to start with the woman he wants to marry."

"I can't believe I'm his first."

"*Fraulein* Stuart, I cannot help what you believe or not, but he's proposed to you. Have you answered him yet?"

"I beg your pardon."

"Krystia's proposed to you. What do you say?"

"Wait a minute." Mariette backed away. "You know, Herr Steiner, this is getting very, very strange—and it's starting to piss me off. You want my answer to Christian's proposal before I give it to him? That's absurd. After all, I would be marrying Christian Stanislaus, right? Not Steiner & Ernesto International."

"*Ja.* My dear departed Alma left instructions. Krystia has to make his own choice and decision, and apparently he's chosen you. I hope you accept because Krystia needs to be married. He needs the love and support of a good woman. That's why I wanted to meet you in person. Now back to business. Who is slandering Krystia? He's my client. I've known him since he was twelve. He's like a little brother to me. Fraulein Stuart, who's telling falsities about Krischan Stanislaus?"

"What? I heard it from someone who knows Christian. They said Christian sleeps around while he's on tour."

"*Never!*"

"Well, they were knowledgeable of the 'circuit' where Christian concertizes."

"*Fraulein* Stuart, this isn't a guessing game. What's the name?

"Mr. Bulter."

"Bulter? Geoffrey Bulter? That nasty little turd! The only thing he knows about Krystia is that he got bested by Krystia in international piano competitions twice. What's he told you?"

"Mr. Bulter told me that Christian's notorious for sleeping around. His reputation is that he tickles as many ladies bottoms as he does piano keys."

"These are lies, Fraulein Stuart. All lies. How do you know Geoffrey Bulter?"

"Last year, he was my music appreciation teacher at University of Cincinnati."

"He told an entire music appreciation class that Krystia slept around?"

"No, no. He just told it to me at the airport when I saw Christian off."

"Did Krystia see him?"

"No. After Christian's plane took off, Mr. Bulter kind of sneaked up and told me."

"*Danke, Fraulein Stuart.* That's what I needed to know. *Auf Wiedersehen.*" Klaus escorted Mariette out of his office and bowed. "*Fraulein* Stuart, it is a pleasure meeting you."

***

After their intimacies, Mariette said, "Klaus came to see me."

"Good. Was he being gracious or cantankerous?"

Mariette sat up. "You and I have a lot to talk about."

Christian wished he were downstairs at the spinet. "All right."

"How did Klaus know you proposed to me?"

"I told him."

"Did you also ask him to ferret out my answer?"

Christian leaned back against the headboard and put his hand on his forehead. *Oh, cuss, Klaus. What did you do? I want the woman to marry me—not be scared off by you.* Christian sat up straight. "I would never do that."

"Why in the world would you tell him?"

"He's my manager."

"You tell him everything?"

He shook his head. "No, not everything."

"Then what things?"

Is getting grilled the prelude to being married? "I wanted to see what he thought of me marrying you."

"You need to ask his permission?"

Apparently it is. "No, I just wanted to apprise him about what I'm considering."

"Which is?"

"I love you, Mariette. I want to marry you. And I would very much like your response."

"Was Klaus supposed to elicit that response out of me?"

"No." Christian shook his head. "Absolutely not." *Dammit, Klaus. What did you ask her?* "I apologize that he did that."

"It seems to me that Klaus should be the one apologizing for himself—not you."

Christian retrieved his handkerchief from the nightstand and dabbed his forehead. "Please understand, Mariette. I have to work very closely with Steiner & Ernesto International. They schedule all my performances, where and when I travel, and where I stay."

"And your part in all this is?"

"My part? I perform. Whatever is required, needed, contracted. I need to be prepared to play anything."

"And if we wed? Where would I fit into this grand little scheme?"

Christian leaned back. *This is going awfully fast. I need to take a moment before I answer this one.* "I want you to be my wife. I want to grow old with you. Have babies. A boy who looks like you, a girl who looks like me. Live in a real house, not some hotel room. Where there's scribbles on the walls because the two-year-old got artistic with a felt pen. Where there's a dog that sheds all over the place and is big enough for the kids to ride. A bathroom that has your swimsuit and panties hanging all over the place. A bed big enough for all of us to have breakfast on Sunday mornings. Mariette, you can fit in wherever you want. Do and be whatever you desire. Skin-diving. Oceanography. Marine biology. Whatever you wish. I just ask that you do it while wed to me. I need you. You don't take me so damned seriously. I need that." He searched her face for some recognition and gently cupped her cheek. "Oh, how I need that. It's very easy for me to take myself too grandly, buy my own image. It's something I try to look out for, but I often fail and buy my own hype. I don't want to grow old and become one of those 'serious' musicians who's really just a pompous ass. You'd never let me get away with that. I need that in my life."

The man can turn into a silver-tongued orator when he wants to. His vivid phrasings tugged at her heart—just as when he told her he loved her and when he proposed—but she wasn't sure she could trust him. What about what Bulter said? What about the awkward interrogation with Klaus Steiner? What was all that about? Mariette was just not sure.

***

When Klaus Steiner arrived at Mariette's apartment, Christian was playing the piano. "How's 'Rach 2' going, Krystia?"

"*Guten Tag,* Klaus. It's getting there." Christian turned around on the piano stool. "I have a bone to pick with you."

"Only one?" Klaus chuckled. "*Was ist das, Krystia?*"

"Why did you ask Mariette about her answer before she gave it to me?"

Eyes down, looking repentant, Klaus said, "*Es tut mir leid.*"

"That makes her think she's marrying Steiner & Ernesto International rather than me. I thought Alma made you swear you'd stay out of it?"

"I said I was sorry."

Christian returned to playing the second movement of Rachmaninoff's "Piano Concerto 2."

"Listen, Krystia. I found something out."

"Which is?"

"Who told her you were being promiscuous?"

"Go on."

"Would you please stop playing for a second and listen?"

Christian stopped playing. "I am listening. I can do that while I play, you know."

"But then you're not concentrating on the playing as well as you should. Are you?"

Christian turned around, looked directly into Klaus's eyes. "So, who or what is it?"

"That nasty little turd, Geoffrey Bulter."

"Bulter? Why?"

Klaus Steiner poked around his coat pocket for his package of walnuts, popped one into his mouth, and plopped down on the sofa. "Think about it, Krystia. What do you want more than anything?"

Right now? To be left alone to work out the second movement of "Rach 2."

Klaus continued, "Mariette Stuart, right? Bulter's keeping that away from you just like you kept the Leeds and Liszt awards away from him."

Christian went back to playing "Rach 2." Suddenly, he stopped and turned back to Klaus. "After all these years? Why?"

"Some people never forgive or forget. I think we just ran into one of those."

"At Mariette's expense?"

"*Nein!* At *your* expense."

Christian shook his head, turned back to the keyboard, and buried himself in Chopin's "Revolutionary Étude."

Klaus Steiner leaned over and grasped Christian's shoulder. "Revolt on your own time, Krystia. Go back to 'Rach 2.' I have you booked to play it in three months."

"Oh, yeah, Klaus," Christian snapped. "That's really good. No pressure, right?"

"I'm sure you'll be ready. You always are. I have all confidence."

"All right, all right. Who and where?"

"Masterson, San Diego."

"Rory? I'm playing with the San Diego Symphony Orchestra and Rory Masterson conducting?"

"*Ja,* I thought you'd be pleased."

"*Ja, ich bin.* I am. Only three months, huh?" Christian waved Klaus away. "*Auf Wiedersehen*, Klaus. *Verlassen.* Leave."

As Klaus Steiner left, he chortled. *That'll keep him busy.*

***

After their intimacies, Mariette balanced herself on her elbow. "When I saw Klaus the other day, he told me something about you that really surprised me."

Christian looked down at his fingernails. "Are you going to tell me or am I supposed to guess?"

"Do you remember when we first had relations in your suite?"

Christian leaned against the headboard and glanced down at her. "I do."

"Yes. Was that the first time you'd done that?"

Christian shook his head and shrugged. "First time I'd done what?"

"Take a woman to bed."

So that's where she's going with this. "I know you think I bed every woman I can find, but I don't. You're the first and only."

"So, you've only had *intimacies* with me."

"Had to start somewhere—so I started with the woman I want to marry."

"That's exactly what Klaus said."

"It's always said to steal from the best. So, I do."

"How did you know what to do?"

His forehead wrinkled. "How did I know what to do about what?"

"Make love. If that was your first time, I would imagine you would be awkward."

Christian looked down, sighed, and shrugged. "I don't know. I guess I just did what I thought felt good and what I thought would make you feel good."

"Oh."

"Was I mistaken?"

"Not at all." She shook her head. "You were quite masterful."

Christian moaned. "Mariette, please don't say that. The next thing I'm going to hear from you is that I must practice often to be so masterful. And I don't. The only thing I practice daily is my piano."

"Grete Steiner did say you were married to your piano."

"Please believe her."

***

Christian was slicing eggplant at the kitchen island.

Mariette watched him deftly slice half-inch cuts. "Christian, when I saw you for the first time, you were doing something that I thought was a little contrived."

He dredged the eggplant slices in flour on both sides and dipped them into the olive oil in the heated frying pan. "Which was?"

"Women were asking you questions, and you paid rapt attention to each question. In response, you fed back to them what they had just said. Do you remember that?"

He stirred red sauce in a pot, tore fresh basil leaves, and tossed them in. He whisked again and took the kettle off the flame. "Well, mostly I remember that I was very jet-lagged from my tour, but that would be the procedure I'd follow. It's a device I use."

"What do you mean device?"

"It's a technique that makes a person feel his or her question is astute when I give them my full attention. And when my answer agrees with them, they like me. People like it when you agree with them." He turned over the browned slices of eggplant.

"So, you do realize you do that?"

"Yes, I know I do it." Christian ladled red sauce into a greased casserole and placed browned eggplant slices on top. "When I'm in a jet-lagged state, it's something convenient to fall back on."

"Don't you think that's a little contrived?"

He pushed a bowl of grated mozzarella into her hands. "Here, help. Put a couple of handfuls of cheese on the eggplant."

"Yes, sir."

"Mariette, I'm a musician. A performer. Just about everything I do is devised to have people like me and like my music. When people like me, it sells tickets, CDs, records, whatever I'm hawking to keep my career alive."

She sprinkled the shredded mozzarella on the eggplant. "Isn't that manipulating people?"

He grated Parmigiano-Reggiano cheese. "I don't manipulate anyone. I interpret the music as best as I possibly can. Hopefully, it satisfies the audience—but they are free to do whatever they want. I play the best I can so they choose me."

"Did Klaus teach you how to do this?"

"Among other things. Klaus also taught me to always be very polite and to always listen. Mariette, I'm not perfect. I mentioned before that there are a lot of chinks in my armor."

"I am getting that picture."

"Good. Now stop grilling me and make yourself useful." He pointed to the casserole. "We need another layer here: red sauce, eggplant, mozzarella, and Parmesan. Then it goes in the oven."

She ladled red sauce atop the eggplant. "And what do you call this dish?"

"Melanzane Parmigiana. Eggplant Parmesan."

"So how does a Ukrainian, Polish, American pianist learn to cook Italian?"

"He likes to cook and knows how to follow directions."

***

Christian held her at bay. "Mariette, I need to stop sharing intimacies with you. It exacerbates the situation. It makes me look like I am sexually promiscuous everywhere I go. That's not true. And you, the woman I love, don't believe me when I tell you the truth. That hurts a lot."

She quickly wrapped her arms around him. "No, Player, don't. I don't want you to do that. I love our intimacies, and I don't want you to cut them off?"

"Mariette, if we married, we could have our intimacies every night."

"Assuming you were in town that night."

"I'll have Klaus cut back on my touring."

She shook her head. "You honestly think Cantankerous Klaus would put up with that? It would definitely cut into his precious manager's cut; 15 percent salary of your pay is a lot of money."

"Klaus will do whatever I want. He works for me; I don't work for him."

"Are you sure he's aware of that?"

"Of course he is. And he gets 20 percent, not 15."

Mariette gasped. "What? You're kidding. Managers usually get 15 percent—not 20 percent." She shook her head. "I've got to take over your finances."

"As soon as you marry me, you can."

"Not just yet."

"Fine! I withdraw my marriage proposal."

"You can't do that," she said.

He walked to the stairway and bounded down the stairs "I just did."

Chopin's "Revolutionary Étude" sounded on the piano.

Mariette sprinted down to the living room, leaped toward the spinet, and slammed her arm down over his knuckles.

The playing stopped.

"Don't you ever do that to me again," she said.

"Excuse me. I'm working," he said.

"No, you're not," she shouted. "You're running to your piano to avoid confrontation. It's just another one of your little 'devices.' Admittedly, it's classier to run away and bury yourself in Beethoven, but you're still running away."

"I'm playing Chopin—not Beethoven."

"I don't care who you're playing. You don't run off in the middle of an argument. You fight it out."

"Mariette? I don't fight."

"No, you just run away and take it to your piano. You bury your head in Beethoven, Chopin, whoever."

"I don't fight. I make music. And the word is *whomever*—not whoever. The word's an object not a subject."

"You little show-off prick!" she shouted. "Is that how you fight? By correcting someone's grammar?"

"I don't want to fight at all," he said quietly. "Playing the piano handles my aggressions."

"You never get aggressive about anything. Don't you care enough to fight?"

"I care enough to play one hell of a 'Revolutionary Étude.'" Christian resumed playing a rambunctious Chopin "Étude."

She pulled his arm, stopping his playing. "So this is it? This is what life with a lily-livered klavierspieler is going to be?"

Christian looked down at his hands and nodded. "I've been called worse. Piano players usually are."

"We have a fight—and you run down to your piano and bang out something appropriate in response. Coward!"

He shrugged. "It's another one of my little chinks. I don't fight."

Mariette shadowboxed punches in front of Christian's face, hoping it would prod his aggressions.

He held up his hands. "Mariette, don't strike me. Please. That jab of yours could fell a mule."

Exasperated, Mariette shook her head. "Christian, you are so full of yourself."

"At times I can be, yes. That's why I need you to tell me to cut the crap."

"You think I'd want to do that for the rest of my life?"

"I think you're dying to do that. Put the old fart in his place."

"That is tempting."

"See? We need each other. Keep me from being a pompous ass."

She shook her head. "Nice try, but no sale, klavierspieler. I'm still not marrying you." She turned and left the room.

***

Klaus Steiner listened intently as he strolled up the walkway to Christian's new studio in San Diego. The studio was empty but for a spinet piano, a sofa, and Christian Stanislaus. He wore a pair of blue jeans and was rehearsing Rachmaninoff "Piano Concerto 2."

"When were you going to tell me that you moved in here?"

Christian glanced up. "Klaus, you're so omniscient. I didn't see the point. I knew you'd figure it out on your own."

"When did you move in?"

"This morning," Christian replied. "Now get out of here. I'm working." He resumed playing.

"'Rach 2' section 2 is played adagio—not lento. What you're playing sounded absolutely funereal."

Christian shrugged. "That's a matter of opinion."

Klaus sighed. "What's wrong? Seeing as you've moved out, I gather there's troubles with Mariette?"

"I guess." Christian wiped his brow. "I unproposed last night."

"You what?"

Christian looked up from his keyboard. "I withdrew my proposal of marriage to Mariette Stuart."

"You can't do that."

"I can't? And this is you following Alma's instructions about not interfering in my life?"

"Calm down, Krystia," Klaus said. "Take a deep breath. Let it out slowly. Now tell me what happened between you and Mariette."

"I don't know, Herr Doktor. I guess I lost my temper."

"*Ah.* The rare occasion when Krystia Stanislaus loses his temper. As I recall, they're very few and far between but extremely memorable—even years later." Klaus ambled over to the sofa and plopped down. "Continue. I want the details. *Bitte.*"

Christian paused and tried to compose himself. *It all happened so quickly. The last thing I remember clearly was the difficulty of getting the spinet through the studio door.* "Mariette wanted the intimacies, but she's refused to marry me. I lost it and withdrew my proposal. Then I went downstairs and banged out my frustrations on the spinet."

Klaus snorted. "Oh, I'm sure she loved that."

"No, actually, she didn't. She ran downstairs and slammed her arm down on my knuckles so I'd stop playing."

Klaus stood, walked over and wrapped his arm around Christian's shoulders. He said, "Oh, Krystia. You've got a lot to learn about being married. You can't issue an ultimatum and run off to your piano, ignoring her."

Christian shrugged off the embrace. He turned to Klaus with a pained look. "She still thinks I screw around on her, and I don't. And it hurts a whole lot that she doesn't believe me."

"Welcome to being married, my friend."

Christian groaned. "But I'm not married to her. That's the whole point."

Klaus dismissed Christian's whine with a shrug. "Well, you can always view the situation this way. You don't have to marry the cow—and you're getting the milk for free."

Christian's head snapped back. "Klaus! That's the crudest, most vulgar thing I've ever heard you say." He leaped up and pointed to the door. "Get out of my studio, right now. *Auf Wiedersehen.*"

"*Ah, Krystia. Ich entschuldige mich.*"

"Keep your lousy apology to yourself, Klaus. Just go."

"You've got it really bad, don't you?"

"I don't know what I've got," Christian snapped. "But I don't have her."

"*Mein Gott!*" Klaus lifted his hands. "And I've got a lovesick *klavierspieler* on my hands."

"Klaus, this really isn't the time." Christian pointed toward the door. "Let me work out my problems with 'Rach 2.' *Bitte. Weiter.* Go!"

Chapter 20

Klaus Steiner drove to Via Excelencia Business Park and entered Steiner & Ernesto International's San Diego office. The six-thousand-square-foot office was furnished with walnut floors, cabinets, and furnishings and Aubusson rugs. "*Grete, Liebchen.* I'm back."

Grete Steiner appeared from a back room, glanced at her father, and shook her head. "Ah, Papa, which client's the problem, now?"

"How do you know there's a problem?" Klaus walked to the side bar and poured himself a large mug of coffee.

"Because you look like the stock market is in free fall." Grete watched her father pour the rest of a bottle of schnapps into his coffee. "Judging by that heavy shot of schnapps this early in the morning, I assume Krischan Stanislaus is giving you problems." Grete walked over to the side bar, picked up the empty coffee pot, and set it up again.

Klaus leaned over and kissed his daughter's cheek. "As always, *Liebchen,* you are right."

"What's Krischan done now?" Grete wiped down the bar, threw away the empty bottle of schnapps, and replaced it with another.

"Unproposed to the woman he wants to marry."

Grete snorted. "Did you tell him that's not the way to go about it?"

"He knows," Klaus said. "He's just being stubborn and trying to force a response."

Grete shook her head. "Well, let's see how this turns out. If nothing else, Krischan's always creative. Obstinate but creative."

Klaus pulled a notebook out from his jacket pocket and handed it to his daughter. "I want all these people in my office presently: Krystia, Fraulein Stuart, und that nasty little turd, Geoffrey Bulter."

Grete opened the book and read the names. "Papa, Geoffrey Bulter is not one of our clients."

Klaus Steiner swigged fully from his coffee cup. "Just get him here, *bitte*. Make it sound like we're scouting."

"Are we scouting for new clients?" Grete asked.

"*Nein*," Klaus shook his head vigorously. "And if we were, we certainly wouldn't lure the likes of Geoffrey Bulter. Steiner & Ernesto International stands for quality—not mediocrity."

"Whatever you're up to, Papa, sounds devious. Very devious."

***

Christian approached Grete Steiner's reception desk and politely bowed. "*Guten tag,* Grete. You're looking well."

Grete pointed to Christian and pointed down the hallway.

"No small talk today, eh?"

Grete pointed down the hallway again.

"Grete, you are getting as enigmatic as your father. I gather I'm supposed to go down the hallway."

Grete nodded. "*Viel Gluck.*"

"Good Luck? *Mein Gott.* I'm going to need luck in there, huh? Curiouser and curiouser."

The last time he had been "summoned" to the San Diego office was ten years ago—the day of the Lucia LaTempesta *mit* straight razor incident. He hoped this "summons" would be less bloody.

"Klaus, what's all this about?" Out of the corner of his eye, he noticed Mariette. He turned and bowed. "Mariette, it's good to see you."

Klaus said, "Now we wait."

***

Klaus Steiner paced in front of Mariette Stuart, Christian Stanislaus, and Geoffrey Bulter. They stood, nervously wondering when the shoe would drop.

"Klaus, what's—"

Klaus's open palm faced toward Christian Stanislaus shut him up.

"I am very, very displeased," Klaus announced.

"And I should care about that?" Geoffrey Bulter asked.

"*Ja,* you should because I can retaliate and make your lives very, very uncomfortable."

"Bullshit," Geoffrey Bulter continued. "How can you possibly touch me?"

"By putting out a lot of bad press," Klaus Steiner said. "Calling in a lot of favors and making any jobs having to do with pianos and music disappear for you, *Herr Bulter.*"

Klaus turned to Christian Stanislaus.

Christian held up his hands in surrender. "You don't have to convince me, Klaus. I know you could make my life sheer hell."

"Would I do that to you, Krystia?" Klaus patted him on the shoulder.

"And what about me, Herr Steiner?" Mariette Stuart asked. "How will you make my life uncomfortable?"

Klaus shook his head. "You, my dear, have already done that to yourself. You make yourself miserable by not having Krischan Stanislaus in it to give you the love *und* the *kinder* you so desire. Now we get back to you, Herr Bulter."

"You can do nothing to me," Bulter said. "Your threats are empty."

"You can believe that if you want, but don't forget to check your messages when you get home."

Geoffrey Bulter stepped back. "Then what do you want? Why am I here?"

"*Herr Bulter*, you're here to apologize to *Fraulein Mariette* for all the falsities you told her regarding Krischan Stanislaus."

"Falsities?" Mariette cried out. "What falsities? Mr. Bulter's been feeding me lies these past months?"

Klaus Steiner nodded.

Mariette said, "Falsities? Is that true, Mr. Bulter? Is that why you keep popping up wherever I move—bothering me, stalking me—just to lie to me?"

"Oh, Miss Stuart, you make it so easy. Such a needy person."

Mariette said, "Mr. Bulter, you leave Player and me alone!"

Bulter chortled. "I just wanted to mess with his head." Bulter tipped his head toward Christian Stanislaus. "And the best and quickest way to do that is through you, Miss Stuart."

Christian moved toward Bulter to protect Mariette.

"You are such a naïf, Miss Stuart," Bulter said. "You're always fearing bad news regarding Stanislaus, so you believe anything."

"Yeah, well, believe this." Mariette rapidly struck Bulter in his Adam's apple and face, breaking his nose.

Christian wrapped his hand around Mariette's fist. "That's enough, *Liebchen. Bitte.*"

On the Aubusson rug, Bulter wiped his bloody nose.

Klaus rushed to his desk and picked up the intercom. "Grete, contact Ernesto. Get him over here *schnell*. And please bring some towels in here to soak up the blood on the Aubusson. Thank goodness the base color of the rug is red."

***

After Bulter left in an ambulance, Mariette turned to Christian. "Geoffrey Bulter convinced me that you were indiscriminate when you were not. Doesn't that make your blood boil?"

"No." Christian shook his head. "What I find most distressing is that you don't trust me when I tell you the truth. You would believe Geoffrey Bulter rather than me?"

"Player, you have to understand. When I was eighteen years old, my father introduced me to my ex-husband. I was young and fell hopelessly in love with him. I thought he was like my father—an honest family man who was devoted to my mother—but he wasn't. He was like his father who kept his wife in the suburbs while he went into town and fooled around. When I found out, we got into a fight and Robert hit me. I threw him out."

"Go on."

"Then I met you, and our intimacies were so powerful. It was never like that with Robert. I feared and dreaded losing you, especially when you were away for weeks and months at a time. Mr. Bulter tells me that you are notorious for playing around. I was petrified. It could happen all over again. I could be married to another womanizer. I was devastated."

Christian shook his head. "Mariette, I am not promiscuous. And it hurts a whole lot that you think so. I would very much like for you to trust me. But that's something that has to come within you. I can't force it. I can only ask for your trust. *Bitte.*

I hope you can find it in your heart. Be well, *Liebchen*." He nodded to Klaus Steiner and left the room.

***

Klaus told Mariette where Christian Stanislaus was holing up. After being given the street name, Mariette only had to walk up the street and listen for his piano. Mariette scurried up the pathway to the little studio and knocked. "Christian! It's Mariette. Is this a bad time?"

The playing stopped, and the door opened. Mariette and Christian gazed at each other. Their magnetic charm was ignited again.

Christian smiled and held out his hand. "My name is Christian Stanislaus. How do you do?"

Mariette beamed and took his hand. "I'm Mariette Stuart, and I'm doing just fine."

Christian moved aside, allowing access to the tiny workroom. With a wave, he motioned her inside. "Please come in."

"Are we starting from the beginning?"

He nodded. "Seems like a good thing to do. It's something I'd like to do."

"I agree." Mariette walked around the room, noting its well-used couch, spinet, and sheet music piled high. "What a dreary little place," Mariette uttered.

"It's just a studio I rent."

"Where are you living?" Mariette wondered. "Aside from on the road."

"Here. The couch opens up."

"Opens up? It looks like it's already devoured a few people."

"Mariette, I do miss your irreverent, quirky sense of humor." Christian gazed into her for the first time in months. "May I ask a question?"

Mariette snuggled into the corner of the droopy sofa. "Ask away."

"Would you honor me with your presence at my concert Saturday night?"

His face was gaunt with fatigue, and his eyes were black with passion. She knew the look. Mariette had never been to one of his concerts. She wanted to see all the theatrics. Mariette laughed. "My pleasure."

"I can't accompany you—unless you care to hang around a dressing room a few hours before the concert begins. I will arrange for two seats though if you care to have someone accompany you."

"I can get there on my own, thank you very much. And I only need one seat because I expect you to take me home."

"Certainly. One more favor?"

"Yes."

"You don't know what it is yet. I may be way out of line in asking."

"I was saying yes—ask the favor. Then I'll tell you if it's out of line or not."

"Saturday night. Do you think you could wear—" He bit his lip. "If this is too presumptuous, just say so."

"Don't worry. If it is, I will."

"That red dress. You know, the one that's—"

His hands fluttered around his throat, silhouetted a buxom chest, and his index finger traced a line up the side of his leg to his hip. "You wore it the time we dined at the castle in San Francisco."

"The dragon lady dress?"

"Is that what you call it?"

"The one with the black dragons?"

"Yes, that one."

"I didn't know you liked that dress." Luckily, she hadn't thrown it away in her move. Not holding such good memories, she almost had.

"Oh, yes. Very much."

"All right, done. I'd be happy to wear it for you." She bent forward to kiss his temple. Her eyes caught his skewed brow. The angle of the light touched his forehead and shined through the hairs of the brow, illuminating the scar. About a quarter-inch thick, it was jagged and ran the length of his brow. She bent down and softly kissed it.

He pulled away in surprise. A brief look of horror flashed across his face as he looked down at her hands and back into her eyes.

"Did I hurt you?"

Smiling once again, he shook his head. "No. Just startled me."

"How'd it happen? Cutting onions?"

"Excuse me?"

"The scar in there. Looks pretty nasty. How'd you get it?"

"Oh, accident. Ran into a brick wall."

"Oh." Mariette wondered why he wouldn't tell her about it.

Chapter 21

On the evening of January 20, the San Diego Symphony Orchestra performed Mozart's "Symphony No. 32 in G, K. 318," Beethoven's "Symphony No. 1 in C," and Rachmaninoff's "Piano Concerto No. 2 in C minor." Rory Masterson was the conductor, and Christian Stanislaus played piano. The performance started at 8:30. At 8:15, Mariette Stuart was in her seat—front row, loge, stage left.

Mariette wore the dragon lady dress, black *peau de soie* high-heeled shoes, and a black taffeta stole. Her raven tresses hung soft and loose around her shoulders. The night's warmth and humidity had put the perfect touch of waviness in her locks. A pristine white hibiscus pinned a few tresses back above her left ear. She looked perfect, if she thought so herself.

She flipped through the program. Unable to concentrate on the brief history of the symphony or the curriculum vitae of the conductor, she closed the booklet. She opened it again to see if there was anything written about Player. There was an insert with a short bio and an atrocious picture of him tucked at the end of the program. She closed it again. There was nothing in it about him she didn't already know. She looked at her watch. It was 8:30. She wondered if these things started on time.

The musicians started strolling onto the stage. Violinists sat on either side the conductor's podium and started tuning their instruments. The violists, cellists, and bass players positioned themselves behind the violins. Flautists and oboists wandered in, arranging themselves to the rear of the strings and tested their reeds and mouthpieces. String instrumentalists, brass, and horns tootled or fiddled on their own—with no regard for the others. The percussion players came in last, standing guard behind their timpani and cymbals. There was no sleek black concert grand piano with Bösendorfer written in gold on the side. Where was that being limbered up on?

As the cacophony of orchestral tuning intensified, Mariette's heart beat faster. She held her breath as the lights dimmed.

When Rory Masterson bounded onto the stage, the audience wildly clapped. He smiled at the audience, turned, and went over to the podium. The orchestra immediately silenced and sat erect. A pin dropping could've been heard. No one in the audience so much as coughed. Rory surveyed the orchestra from one side of the stage to the other. Facing toward the rear of the stage, he raised his arms. His hands were clenched in fists. He made a quick thrust out with his fingers, and the orchestra began.

Mariette wriggled to the edge of her seat. As the Mozart symphony played, she studied the musicians' faces. They were somber and intense. With eyes up, they beheld their conductor. Eyes down, they stared at sheets of paper in front of them—while performing amazing tactile manipulations on their instruments. She watched Rory Masterson waving his arms and hands. The resulting sound of all this movement astounded Mariette. It was not the sound of the music that captivated her but how all the parts came together as a whole.

She squirmed in her seat. This was exciting. She could get to like concerts.

At the end of the music, the crowd clapped madly. Several people in the audience stood up and shouted, "Bravo!"

Rory, who'd deserted the stage at the end of the piece, raced back and took a bow. The ovation thundered. Turning to his orchestra, Rory motioned for them to stand. Like a hundred soldiers, they rose in unison. With a sweep of his left hand, the orchestra bowed. The audience went silly with applause and cheers. When Rory went back to the podium and the audience settled down, Mariette was surprised to find herself on her feet cheering.

The next selection was Beethoven's "Symphony No. 1." Mariette was getting antsy. Her agitation was overwhelming. She felt like a child on Christmas Eve. The anxiety would build until she passed out from exhaustion, but she had no intention of swooning in the audience at Player's concert. His appearance was taking so long.

Imagining herself in the ocean, she took the same slow, deep breaths she used on her oxygen tank respirator. She concentrated on each breath. Closing her eyes, she gradually calmed. With the music playing in the background, her breathing became pleasurable. Being in the hall became enjoyable. Abruptly, the music stopped. Everyone stood and cheered again.

Mariette opened her eyes and looked around. The lights had come on fully. The audience noise dwindled to a low murmur. Intermission had arrived. People moved to the lobby. Mariette remained seated and watched the curtains. When they swept open, Player's piano was right in front of the podium. Looking at her watch, Mariette wondered what Player did all this time.

***

In his dressing room, Christian Stanislaus paced. His palms sweated. His nerves twitched. He couldn't believe it. He wasn't scared; he was petrified. Not since Maestro Lochner first sat in the audience at one of his concerts had he felt so jumbled. And for what? That 110-pound girl with the impish smile and compelling green eyes? He grabbed the glass of water on his dressing table. Taking a gulp of water and a swallow of air at the same time, he started to choke. The coughing continued until he sat down and calmed himself enough to inhale deeply and slowly as the water passed from his lungs. The thought of her sitting out there was more than enough to rattle him. In fact, it made his stomach lurch. Even command performances and recitals for heads of state hadn't affected him like that.

That's it. You're creating this all in your head. Your happiness in life does not depend on this performance swaying that woman. He grabbed his tailcoat, put it on, and paced the hallway. Yes, it did. This was the last trick he had up his sleeve. If this didn't persuade her to marry him, nothing would.

Intermission was over, and the orchestra was in place. Rory Masterson was on his way back to the stage. Seeing Christian pacing the hallway, Rory grabbed his arm. "Hey, partner, you okay?"

Christian glanced up at the behemoth at his side. Rory Masterson was a good two inches taller and wider than Christian. Rory favored wearing a ten-gallon hat with his white tie and tails whenever he was backstage. As one of the most talented up-and-coming young conductors on the music scene, Rory liked it to be known that despite his Juilliard School of Music education, he was still a good old boy at heart and didn't really see why the two couldn't mix.

Rory's mammoth hand squeezed Christian's shoulder. "You're looking a little peaked there."

Christian pulled himself up straight and said, "I'm fine. Thanks."

"Sure you are." Rory pulled Christian to the curtained wings of the stage. "Everyone gets a little skittish now and again. Be a damned fool not to. Besides, I warmed 'em up for you."

Christian chuckled. "Yes, you did. Thank you."

Still out of sight of the audience, Christian deferred to Rory as they approached the stage. Protocol decreed that he follow the conductor's lead. With a wave of his arm, Christian stepped aside, allowing Rory to precede him. "Maestro."

"Mah-A-stroh," Rory repeated. "Mah-A-stroh. I like the way you say that. When I have young ones, I think I'll have 'em call me Mah-A-stroh. It sounds so classy."

Just prior to setting foot on stage, Rory plucked the hat from his head, spun around, and flung it to the stagehand running anxiously toward them. The man leaped into the air and caught the hat. Rory called out, "Thought I'd forget it, didn't ya, Phil?"

Rory walked a few feet onto the stage. The audience burst into applause. He turned around and gave a thumbs-up to Christian.

As Rory went to the podium, a mellifluous voice announced, "Conductor Masterson is returning to the podium. He will be joined by Christian Stanislaus at the piano in a performance of the 'Piano Concerto No. 2 in C Minor' by Serge Rachmaninoff."

Mariette's stomach fluttered as Christian walked onto the stage. Even though she sat above him, looking down from on high, Christian looked larger than life. He was beautiful in his cutaway coat. His legs were long and lithe in the formal trousers with satin seams. The white bow tie made him look distinguished and very sexy. Gulping hard, Mariette started to perspire. She was so nervous, which was funny since she doubted he was. That man was always too contained to yield to something as mundane as nervousness.

Christian sat at the piano, rested his hands on the lip of the keyboard shell, and stretched his legs to within reach of the pedals. Nodding slightly to the conductor, he lowered his eyes to the keyboard. The first notes he played were chords that sounded like a bell tolling. String instruments swept over him with a melancholy tune. Christian played with and against the strings until he finally countered them by playing a lush, more melodic second tune. The strings played around and against Christian's melody until he finally grabbed their theme and pounded it forcefully out on his piano. Horns joined in next, taking Christian's original melody and playing it sweetly and lovingly until Player took his melody back, putting it to rest with even more force.

Mariette loved watching Christian's face as he played. It was alternately tender and fierce and loving and vicious. But mostly it was all Player: his expressions, his gestures, his charm. *So, this is what he meant by making the music his?* The more she listened, the more swept up in his playing she became. *I know this man. I know what he's doing down there. And he's right. He would be miserable if he couldn't do this.*

The second movement started with Christian playing against the strings. His sound was dreamy and romantic. When an oboe came in to play opposite him, their music was conversation, mostly dulcet but occasionally beseeching. After one forceful assertion, Christian's music returned to wistful playing. His face grew pensive as he responded to the strings.

With the third movement, fiery music alternated with calm, sweeping sounds as Player and the oboes and violas whirled around one another. A cymbal added occasional punctuation.

161

Mariette opened her eyes. Christian was in the midst of a studied resurgence of his original tune. She could see the passion in his eyes. She smiled at her secret knowledge of his passion. Right then, she decided she wanted no one else to know that passion of his as intimately as she. He had given it to her and her alone. She wanted it to stay there forever. The concerto finished with both the piano and orchestra heralding the second theme. The audience erupted in applause. Everyone leaped to their feet and cheered.

It seemed to her an eternity that Christian remained seated at his piano. He stared at the keyboard as if fathoming what he'd just done. Suddenly, he walked over to the conductor, briefly pumping Masterson's hand, and did the same with the violinist closest the conductor. Christian walked to the apron of the stage. Starting on the right side, he acknowledged and analyzed the audience as he bowed. He did the same with the center section. When his appreciation reached the left section where Mariette was seated, his gaze passed over her, caught her eye, and looked back.

Everyone in the house was standing. At the moment his eyes caught sight of her, Mariette lifted her arm above her head. Mariette had trusted the engagement ring would still be in the safety-deposit box because he promised it would— Christian always kept his promises—and it was. Mariette's left hand was angled toward the stage as she applauded. The distance between the loge and stage was far enough for her to question if he could see her clearly. She knew he'd caught sight of the emerald engagement ring on her finger when he came to a dead stop.

Gazing up at the balcony, he backed up a few steps. His eyes widened, and his mouth dropped. A sudden smile and quiet laugh shook through him as he looked up at her. Bending down from the waist with his left hand over his heart and his right arm circling behind him, he executed the courtliest bow she could ever imagine. Unaware of the reason for such gallantry, the audience nonetheless roared their approval.

A sudden impulse swept through Mariette. She unpinned the hibiscus in her hair and tossed it down to him. Christian beamed and caught the flower as it floated toward him from above. The crowd cheered and called for an encore, over and over until Christian obliged with an impassioned "La Campanella." Ecstasy swept Mariette. Viewing Christian playing her favorite piece was more fulfilling than she'd imagined. His fired playing on the Animato far surpassed all her expectations. His Liszt piece completed, Christian took two curtain calls and left the stage.

Mariette stood in shock. The sheer magnetism of Player's performance was awesome. She was shaking from it. An usher asked if she were Miss Stuart and instructed her to kindly follow him. They wound through a maze of stairs and hallways until she arrived backstage.

The scene backstage was a crush of audience trying to get in, musicians trying to get themselves and their instruments out, and the stage-door guard playing referee. Mariette was astonished by all the confusion and bustle. She immediately lost track of the usher and tried to find Christian in the crowd.

As she listened through the levels of clamor backstage, a woman's breathy voice said, "Oh, Mr. Stanislaus? Could you please sign my program? You were so marvelous tonight."

Turning toward the voice, Mariette searched the crowd until she honed in on its source. A tall, leggy blonde about ten feet away rested her hand on Christian's forearm. He accepted her program while delicately removing the woman's hand. Bending, he said something to her, she replied, and he signed the program.

The blonde inched closer to Christian. "You know, Christian. May I call you Christian? I've been watching your career. I even caught your concert in Frankfurt in December."

Christian surveyed the crowd as the woman talked. His gaze found Mariette. Mariette watched as Christian grinned. Without so much as a glance to the woman at his side, he mumbled, "Excuse me."

The next second, Mariette had Christian's arms around her. His forearms supported her in an embrace as he leaned her back for a kiss. The kiss was long, deep, and wonderfully wet.

Christian pulled back from her, his eyes searching her face as he kept her suspended in space.

"Oh, my love." Mariette gasped and offered her mouth again.

With a ragged groan, Christian crushed his mouth to hers.

"Bravo!" someone drawled. It was accompanied with slow clapping. The applause came nearer. The angle that Christian was holding Mariette and the duration of the kiss was putting on quite a show. Mariette didn't care. He was hers now.

"Nice encore," the voice continued.

Christian righted them both. Keeping an arm draped over Mariette's shoulder, he turned toward the intruder.

Rory Masterson stopped clapping. With a broad grin, he looked at Christian and said, "Oh, the one on the stage was good too."

"Mariette, this is the conductor, Rory Masterson. Rory, this is my … fiancée?"

She nodded and smiled.

"This is my fiancée, Mariette Stuart."

"Fiancée?" Rory's eyes ravaged Mariette from her widow's peak to her toes. Stripping his cowboy hat from his head and holding it to his chest, he bent low. He lifted her left hand to his lips and kissed it. "Ma'am, as pretty as that ring is, it pales in comparison to you." He turned to Christian and said, "So this is why you were wearing ruts in the carpet earlier." His gaze found Mariette once again. "Yeah, she'd unnerve me too."

Mariette looked at Christian and chuckled. So he'd been nervous as well.

"Oh, and such a delightful laugh!" Rory continued. "May I kiss the future Mrs. Stanislaus?"

Fierce with protective pride, Christian tightened his arm around Mariette's shoulder. He looked Rory dead in the eye. "No."

Rory backed down. "Sorry, old man. But if you're going to marry someone this beauteous, you're going to have to get used to men at least trying. So, where are we going for a little late-night excitement?"

"Well," Christian said. "I'm taking Mariette to Del Coronado to celebrate our engagement." With a wicked grin, he added, "I don't know where you're going."

Rory turned to Mariette. "Watch him, little lady. He's got a nasty jealous streak in him."

Mariette looked at Christian and said, "Oh, I trust him— he has nothing to fear."

"Wooh! I'd marry her too if she said sweet words like that to me. Hotel Del Coronado, eh? That's the fancy little place on the Naval Island. Hangout for all the movie stars during the thirties. Nah! Too sedate for me. I need to kick up my heels. You two go and have fun." Rory looked around at the deserted backstage. "Well, I better be blowin'. See ya next time you're passing through." He tipped his hat to Mariette. "It was certainly a pleasure meeting you, ma'am." He slapped Christian on the shoulder. "Take good care of her, buddy."

At the stage door, Rory turned. "Invite me to the wedding—if you dare."

Mariette couldn't keep from laughing as Rory ambled away. "The man is persistent."

"Rory? Yes, very, but I like him. He's an original." Christian released Mariette's shoulders and claimed her hand. "Come on. I have a limousine waiting to take us to Coronado."

Chapter 22

The ride to Coronado was over a long bridge across San Diego Bay. In the darkened backseat of the limousine, Mariette snuggled close to Christian.

"You really are incredible at what you do," Mariette said as Christian nuzzled her neck. "Not just your playing but the whole performance. If I wasn't already in love with you, I would be now."

Shocked, Christian pulled away from her neck. He pointed to her. He pointed to himself. He mouthed the words: *You love me?*

Mariette nodded. "Oh, didn't I tell you?"

Christian slowly shook his head.

"Oh. It must have slipped my mind. But you're so self-confident, I figured you already know."

"I am not that self-confident. I do like hearing such things."

"Good! Then let me go on. You were marvelous tonight. What you did gave me gooseflesh. When you walked out onto the stage, you looked so comfortable and in control—"

He leaned forward and kissed her into silence. "Yes, I know. I was stupendous. Now, hush up and kiss me back."

"Wait a minute!" She untangled herself and pulled from his arms. "You said you wanted to hear these things. I'd never been to one of your concerts before. I think it is important for you to know how exciting it was to see you on that stage."

The blood rushed to Christian's head. He felt his face burning, his body tingling, and his mouth drying. He couldn't believe it. Her words were embarrassing him. Not since Lindy Miller stood up in front of the entire fourth grade class to announce that Christian Stanislaus was the only boy in all of Hoover Elementary School worth kissing had he felt so chagrined.

"The power you exude, the magnetism—"

"Mariette, if I knew you were going to fall like some Stage-Door Dolly, I would have played for you when I first met you and gotten this all over with."

Mariette stopped talking and sat back. He sounded so flustered and so beside himself as he spoke. She studied his profile as he watched the back of the driver's head. If the limousine hadn't been so dark, she'd swear he was blushing. Her words were embarrassing him. She couldn't believe it. All at once, sitting next to her wasn't the debonair musician who'd just brought Symphony Hall to its feet. It wasn't the self-made man who'd taken the risks and succeeded. It was the piano tuner's son caught sneaking piano lessons, the boy who fretted he'd be banished when Maestro tattled to his father. The thought tickled her. Then the amusement faded. A strange thought dawned. *This man was wary of what his talent and luck had wrought. He was caught in his own well-calculated trap. He was desperate to have someone understand and share the rarefied air he breathed.*

Mariette gently took his hand and cradled it. "No, you wouldn't have. Because you wanted me to see Christian Stanislaus, the piano tuner's son with all his foibles and peculiarities. Not Christian Stanislaus, the virtuoso pianist who can sweep a woman off her feet just by playing for her."

Christian started to speak.

She stopped him by placing her fingers softly to his lips. Clouds lifted from her eyes. She could see it all clearly now. She felt no confusion. Everything was laid out before her, plain as could be. As the pieces fell into place, Mariette said. "That's how I know you really do care for me. Sweeping me off my feet by playing your piano in concert would have been easy for you, but in your eyes, it was not worth anything. You want someone who understands the boy from Clement Street and isn't awed by him."

Listening to her words, Christian balked. He wasn't the cocksure virtuoso or the immigrant's son. He was a rational, mature balance somewhere in between the two. *Face it, Krystia. No matter what she calls you, that is what you've been doing: showing her the bad with the good and not just the stage strutting.* The lady did have him pegged. He wondered when the young girl he'd been captivated by had turned into such the sagacious woman he was now hearing. And he wondered what had taken her so very long to get here.

The limousine pulled up to the entrance of Hotel Del Coronado. A doorman rushed to open the car door. Christian extricated himself and held out his hand to Mariette as she emerged.

Her hand wrapped around Christian's extended arm, and they strode up the steps. The heavy wooden doors were open wide for them.

Stopping at the threshold, Christian turned to Mariette. "Ready?"

Mariette nodded, and they entered. All heads turned as the handsome couple promenaded through the lobby. Being escorted to the hotel bar, Mariette lifted her head to Christian. "Do you always strut through hotel lobbies in full formal dress?"

"Only when there's a gorgeous woman on my arm."

"How often is that?"

"First time. That's why I'm so awkward at it."

Mariette's appealing laugh infected the entire bar. "I think we've been together too long. Your dialogue is going into reruns."

"Observant woman. I'll have to watch myself."

She loved the verbal sparring he could lure her into. "No. That's my job now."

A hostess arrived. He ordered them both Armagnac, heated.

Mariette sat back in her chair. It felt as if every eye in the room focused on the tall, handsome man in his elegant tailcoat and his stunning brunette companion in her oriental silk brocade evening dress. Casually perusing the crowd, she found she was right. Some people were bending their heads together as they surreptitiously glanced toward them. Whispers buzzed around the room, questioning who the couple was. Some even mentioned Christian's name and Symphony Hall.

Christian looked so content in his chair, keeping the snifter warm in the palm of his hand while attending to her. So this was Player's world? Knock-'em-dead concerts in the evening followed by cocktails and supper at some posh place at night. She could get used to some of that—as long as it wasn't her whole life.

"So what foibles of mine have you found that you think you can life with," he asked.

"Or perhaps *influence?*"

"I wouldn't count on that. At thirty-six, I'm fairly set in my ways."

"Fairly. But you're always looking for improvement. It's the perfectionist in you." Her smile was slow and intoxicating.

His was openly sensual.

She reached across the table and touched his hand. "Well, you're downright immature when it comes to money. But we've already discussed that. And if you don't mind, I do want to oversee the finances. That analyst you have is taking you to the cleaners. I saw your financial statement that he sent. Very sloppy. The man is either very unprofessional or he's purposefully cloaking what he's doing in layers of confusion."

"That's fine. I'm not wed to the man. What else?"

"You're stubborn and very determined."

Christian chuckled. "I told you that."

"Yes, I know, but I thought you were just being patient and biding your time. Now I see that once you set your mind to something, you'll do anything to achieve it."

"Anything?"

"Pretty near. You're no quitter once you make up your mind."

"I was darn close to giving up this time," he teased. "If my performance tonight hadn't swayed you, I just may have."

Batting her eyes at him, she leaned forward and rested her hand on his knee. "Nonsense. That would have been a minor frustrating setback, but you would have come back with a vengeance."

He stretched out his legs and basked in the glow of firelight and her. "You're right, I would have."

"Did you really think your performance tonight would win me over?"

Christian nodded.

Mariette laughed. "The man does know what he is good at. So, why did you wait so long?"

"For all the reasons you've said. And because you are no Stage-Door Dolly to be wowed with a few Rondos I play on stage. You are a beautifully complex woman. You're worth all the time it takes to win you. And so am I."

Mariette smiled at his first words and coughed unexpectedly on his last. "If I may continue with your foibles, you're also vain and arrogant."

Christian's grin became downright devilish.

"But, I like that in you," Mariette continued. "It's gotten you where you are and keeps you up there."

"So, Liebchen, I very much appreciate your deciding to be my fiancée. Why the change of heart?"

"You know, Christian, I had been worrying that, like Robert, you had *paramours* on the side."

"I remember constantly defending myself every time I came back from being on the road, yes."

"And I was right. You do."

"I do what?" Christian asked.

"You have two *paramours*."

"What?" Christian shook his head.

Mariette leaned closer and whispered, "There's the short, chunky brown one and the long, sleek black one. They've been right under my nose for as long as I've known you. You run to one whenever we have words."

Christian sat back. *What in the world is she saying?*

"You were even with one of them earlier this evening."

"Earlier this evening? This evening I was … oh. I see. A tad anthropomorphic, are we?"

Mariette cocked her head. "Oui!"

Christian continued. "So, my pianos are the *paramours*. The short, chunky brown one is the spinet piano, and the long, sleek black one is my Bösendorfer piano. Clever."

"I knew you'd get it."

"But, dear woman, I need to point one thing out. My Bösendorfer preceded you by a couple of decades. Ergo, technically, I cheat on my Bösendorfer and all the other pianos with you."

"Yes, you do," Mariette said.

"Does that bother you?"

"Not a bit. The two of you make beautiful music together. I was grateful to hear it earlier."

"*Danke*. My pleasure." Christian stood and held out his hand. "My dear, either the brandy or your flattery is making me very warm. I suggest we go somewhere and do something about it."

Surprised, she looked around the room "Back to La Jolla?"

He shook his head and raised his eyes toward the ceiling.

"Aren't we having supper?"

"Later. We'll call up for it. But right now, my self-control is faltering."

"So, we're staying the night?"

"Yes. Now, no more questions. Just come."

***

The old-fashioned suite had small rooms, a cozy fireplace, and papered walls. Their coupling was beautiful. He held himself in control until she begged him to release her from the fire he'd methodically taken all evening to build. Afterward, wrapped warm and content in his arms, Mariette blissfully fell asleep.

Waking a few hours later, Mariette found Christian standing at the window. Both hands on the casement, he stared toward the ocean. The moon was full and shone on his face. She felt an unsettling edginess in him.

Walking up from behind, she wrapped her arms around him. "Hello, my love."

He turned. In the moonlight, his good looks took on harsh angles and shadows. His words came slowly. "Mariette, I need to speak of something. I can't marry you unless you know this about me. Even at the risk of you finding it as repulsive as I do and never wishing to see me again, I must tell you this."

His words stunned her like a slap in the face, but their effect propelled her into a businesslike state.

Taking his hand, she brought him back to the bed. "Let's sit down first. Then you tell me." She sat him at the foot of the bed and pulled up a chair for herself. She sat and patiently waited.

As he stared her, he seemed to be taking her in for what might be one last time. Finally, he said, "I've not been very explicit with you about the previous engagement in which I was involved. And purposefully so."

His speech was getting progressively formal. She knew that he used that device to poke fun at himself and distance himself from whatever pressed in too near. Pulling her chair closer, she wrapped her hands around his. His eyes brooded as she watched.

"The woman I was engaged to—"

"Lucia LaTempesta, the opera singer." She nodded, coaxing him on.

"Yes. I've given the impression we didn't know each other well. That's not true. We spent quite a bit of time together. I was introduced to her family. I would even stay at their home in Milan whenever I played near there. The *melanzane parmesana* I made us the other night? That's her mother's recipe. Mama LaTempesta taught me Milanese-style cooking." He turned toward the window. "I'd braid her hair for her sometimes."

"Lucia or her mother?"

"Her mother." His voice still wandered. "Lucia wasn't much interested in such Old World things as braiding hair. She's too modern. Short, angular haircuts are more her style."

Like sand dunes in the wind, Mariette's calm started to shift. It felt as if Mariette's heart was pumping up into her throat. Anxiously, she stopped him. "Lucia? Did you love her?"

He looked like he was surprised to find her in the same room. He disentangled his hands from hers. Bending forward, he rested his elbows on his knees. He shut his eyes and placed his forehead on his folded hands. When his gaze found her again, he was shaking his head. "No. I loved the time. I loved being young and being the best of the young. I loved beating the stuffing out of the Geoffrey Bulters in life. And I loved that Lucia was also good. And I wanted her to be the best too."

He snorted in disgust or self-disgust. Mariette wasn't sure.

"But she wasn't," he continued. "Bizet's 'Carmen,' she could sing as if it were written for her. She'd become a fetching, sultry Carmen. Her voice could bring down the entire house, but only when it struck her fancy and she applied herself. I would tell her that she could be better. She *should* be better. That I gave my all when I performed. She should too. And if she did, she'd be the best." His voice faded as if he were talking to himself. "But she couldn't or wouldn't. Maybe she was afraid—I don't know of what. Maybe herself. Maybe me."

"Anyway, one day, Lucia and I were in Klaus's office. We had both been told we were in the running for some best new artist of the year awards: her for voice and me for instrumental. That day, we found that I'd been awarded the prize. She hadn't. I rubbed it in by saying something appropriately insensitive to her like, 'It's simple why you don't win, cara mia. I give my all. You don't. I can overwhelm with my sheer charismatic presence. You don't apply yourself so you can't.'"

Mariette's mouth dropped as Christian parodied with brutal realism what must have been those words.

"Yes. I was that insufferably arrogant in those days." He shook his head. "I don't quite remember what happened next. I think I turned to Klaus. He was on my right. I saw something flash in the corner of my left eye. I turned to Lucia just as she yelled, 'Basta!' She was coming at me with a straight razor—one of my own. I used them in those days. I thought it suited the image. I lifted my arm to block her attack. Klaus jerked my arm back down and screamed, 'Don't use the hands.'"

Christian briefly brushed the back of his hand over his left eyebrow as if to push his perspiration and the razor away. He was still for a second, and he turned back to Mariette. "That's how I got this scar. The razor caught me just over my eye." He shook his head to shake out the lie. "There was no brick wall."

Mariette's mind raced as she tried to piece together all he was telling her with what she already knew. "Player? Why would I not want to marry you because of what you just told me?"

"First, I've lied to you. I don't want to build a marriage on lies. Second, I pushed the woman I was once engaged to until she felt it necessary to attack. I don't want to goad people until they satisfy me with what they do. My behavior was despicable. And before you enter into a marriage with me, I need you to know I've been capable of both."

Mariette sighed. "Well, if honesty is one of the subjects here, I have to honestly tell you this. I knew how you got the scar. I knew even before I asked you about it the other night. And what I find despicable about the whole incident is that Lucia attacked you."

He shook his head. "How could you have known?"

"Grete Steiner told me."

"Grete? She was a child at the time. What would she know?"

"Well, some early-childhood memories make an impact. This one she remembered quite well, but she did tell me to get the correct version from you. When you weren't keen on discussing it the other night, I let it go. I figured you'd tell me in your own time. And you have. Grete also said you'd be very noble in the telling and blame yourself for the incident.

You've done that too. She told me not to worry because you aren't dangerous."

Christian shook his head. "You already knew about the accident and how I got the scar?"

"Yes."

"Why would she tell you I wasn't dangerous?"

"Because I asked her. The night you stormed out of the bedroom and pounded on your piano until you collapsed, I remembered what you said about your first meeting Lucia. How it was a free-for-all, plate-throwing brawl. That coupled with the dark look in your eyes when you stormed out of the bedroom. I'd never seen you so distraught. When Grete called the next morning, I asked her if you were dangerous."

"What did she tell you?"

"That of all their clients, you're one of the more benign. And you're so bloody noble that you'd blame yourself for the accident."

Christian breathed in deeply, exhaling with a weighty sigh. "Mariette, the accident was my fault. I'd been pushing Lucia to be the best. I did it because I saw the potential in her. I thought she should fulfill it. When the pressure from me got to be too much, she responded in the only way she knew. She attacked. And she was right in doing so. It was the only way I'd understand, leave her be, and steer clear of the woman for the rest of my days."

"And have you?"

With a shudder, Christian said, "Absolutely."

Mariette smiled. "It sounds as though you're afraid of her."

"Of course I'm afraid of her. She attacked me with a razor. I'd be stupid not to be afraid. Her attack was venomous. I was lucky I didn't lose my eye."

"Did you touch Lucia? Did you have intimacies with her?"

Christian walked to the windows, stopped, and walked back. "Never. Not only did Lucia have no desire to be touched, I had no inclination to do so."

"Klaus said you two hated each other."

Christian shook his head. "No, no. Hate is too strong a word. Hate denotes passion. There was none. Just mutual indifference. Apathy."

Mariette hunted around for more information. "The whole notion doesn't sound like it was very promising."

"No, it wasn't," Christian answered. "It was a foolish scheme. Two people who didn't much care for each other were put in an arranged betrothal. And that 'marriage' was solely for the purpose of benefiting their careers. It was sheer lunacy. And I was too young and stupid to see it. So I let it happen."

Mariette said, "A concept doomed to fail, seems to me."

"Yes. And fail it did."

Mariette took Christian's hand and sat them back on the bed. "So where is she now? Where's Lucia? Do you know?"

"Klaus said she married a fellow in Australia. Occasionally, she performs at the Sydney Opera House."

"Well, good for her."

"I concur," Christian said. "And it's also very reassuring to know she resides in a totally different hemisphere than me."

"And Geoffrey Bulter. What's become of him?"

"Well, his nose is pretty much out of joint—thanks to you—but Ernesto is helping him along."

Christian sat Mariette on his knee. "So what's your decision? Am I too dangerous to wed?"

"Hardly," Mariette replied. "I'd be honored to marry you. You're one in a million."

"No, my dear. We're both much rarer than that."

Epilogue

The sun shone through the louvered windows and into Mariette's eyes. She rolled over in the bed and smiled. *Oh, wonderful. Sunday-morning breakfast in bed.* Opening one eye, she focused on the bedside clock. *Ten? Where is everyone?*

Christian opened the bedroom door and wandered in. "Good morning, my dear. How was your night?"

She wiggled a finger, beckoning him over. Reaching her arms around his neck, she pulled him down for a kiss. "Fine. I'm starved." She looked at his empty hands. "Where's breakfast?"

He nuzzled her neck and kissed her back. "Tiana's bringing it up."

"Tiana? A three-year-old is going to manage the breakfast tray up a long, curved flight of stairs?"

"She said she could do it. I believe her. Besides, she has help. She was strapping a thermos of coffee, one of chocolate, and a tin of maple syrup onto Troubles when I left the kitchen."

"Troubles is her help? That poor dog. I don't know if he's named that for all he's caused or all he's seen." Mariette accepted Christian's offer of a dressing gown. "And where's Nicky?"

"Last I saw he was out in the yard in a scuba mask and swim fins, scaring the birds."

"Why don't you call our son in?"

Christian went over to the window and tapped on it. "I hope you're ready for a colorful breakfast," he said over his shoulder.

"Oh no!" Mariette groaned. "Not purple waffles again."

Opening the window, Christian leaned out and said, "Nicklaus, breakfast. Now." He turned back to his wife. "Purple waffles? Of course not. That was last week." He smiled wickedly. "This week it's blue bunny pancakes."

"Oh my," Mariette sighed. "Do me a favor, love? Lose the food coloring—or put it where our daughter can't reach it. There must have been an entire bottle of red and blue food coloring in last week's batter."

"She's a colorful creative child. I don't want to stifle that."

"True. But you can give it some direction, especially in the kitchen."

A thump on the bedroom door was followed by a bark. "Uh-oh!"

Christian ran to open the door.

Tiana wore pink overalls and a white blouse. Her long blonde locks were held back from her brow with a matching pink ribbon. The breakfast tray she held started to seesaw. Her emerald eyes flashed a panicked look to her father.

Christian immediately bent down and grabbed the tilting tray. "Allow me, mademoiselle."

As Tiana was relieved of her burden, a gigantic brindle-speckled dog bounded past her and leaped onto the bed. Pulling herself to her full size, the little girl said, "Troubles, here!" Instantly, the dog obeyed his mistress, flanking her side and dwarfing her by a good foot and a half.

Mariette surveyed the scene at the foot of her bed. Her daughter was a pretty child with Mariette's eyes and mouth and Christian's intensity and self-possession. Troubles was a huge dog with a massive head and a mouth that always dribbled. He was the ugly offspring of a Great Dane and something that must have been very hairy and prehistoric. With a thunderous bark and a menacing growl, Troubles was the most good-natured canine imaginable. He was absolutely devoted to the little girl next to him, as was the man who towered over them both.

Christian came forward with the breakfast tray and placed it before Mariette. He pulled off the plate cover with a flourish while Tiana explained the menu.

"This morning's breakfast is fresh-squeezed orange juice from the garden. The bacon is crisp this morning. The pancakes are in the shape of bunnies and have blueberries in their eyes and bodies."

"Blueberry pancakes!" Mariette opened her arms toward her daughter. "Sweetheart, that's my favorite."

Tiana ran to the side of the bed and into her mother's arms. She nodded and laughed. "I know. Daddy told me."

Mariette shot Christian a glance and shook her head. *Blue bunny pancakes, indeed.*

Released from her mother's arms, Tiana ran to her father. "Daddy! I thought of something real good for next week. You know how pecan nuts look like deer feet. We can make deer pancakes with pecan feet."

Christian ran his hand over his daughter's hair and squatted next to her. "Darling, that's a wonderful idea, but next week, you're on your own. I won't be here."

Tiana gasped. "Why? Where are you going?"

"I'll be in Europe. I have some concerts to play."

The child's shocked stare went from her father's face to her mother's face and back. "Why?"

Mariette said, "Because every summer for two months, your daddy needs to chase his tail all over Europe. Playing his piano. Eating in strange places. Sleeping in a different hotel every night. All so he can receive the crowd's adulation and feel the love of the masses."

Tiana turned to her father. "Why?"

"To remind myself why I don't do it full-time anymore."

Hugging his neck, she asked, "Why is that, Daddy?"

"Because I would sorely miss seeing you grow up—and that would break my heart."

Nicklaus flopped onto the bed in swim fins, trunks, and a face mask.

Christian placed Tiana on the bed and pointed to the door. "Park the flippers outside, Frogman."

Nicklaus removed the flippers and ran back to the bed. He was a solid, sturdy boy with his father's marvelous looks and her wavy black hair and green eyes. He'd grow up to be a beautifully handsome man if he didn't snuff out his own life with his reckless impetuousness first. He stabbed a pancake with his fork and shoved the whole thing into his mouth.

Mariette said, "Nicky, take the mask off when you eat. You can't breathe and chew at the same time."

"Yes, I can. I can do both. Watch."

Christian leaned across the bed and took the mask off Nicky's face. "No. You'll asphyxiate."

"I'll what?"

"You'll choke."

Tiana crawled over to her brother and put another pancake on his plate. "Nicky, Daddy's going away next week."

"I know. He does that every summer after he's through teaching." Nicky looked at his father. "Can I go this time?"

"No. Maybe next time."

"That's what you said last year."

Christian's gaze went from his son to his wife. "Did I?"

Mariette nodded. After taking a sip of coffee, she added, "And the year before that as well."

"Oh." A few moments later, Christian turned back to his son. "I'll tell you what, Nicklaus. Next summer, I'll take you and your sister and mother with me. I promise."

"Oh, really?" Mariette said.

"Yes, really. There are many places I didn't show you on our honeymoon. And no places I've shown the kids. So, you're getting advance warning. Arrange your schedule accordingly. Don't teach any summer classes at the university. Train whatever muscle-bound hulk you have to take over for you at Stuart's Dive School. And next summer, we'll all go."

Mariette laughed heartily. "Uh-oh. Daddy's being impulsive."

"Impulsive?" Christian asked.

Nicklaus turned to his mother. "Mom, does that mean we won't go?"

"Quite the opposite, Nicky. That means we *definitely* will."

With breakfast finished, Mariette noticed her husband's eyes were starting to darken. "Nicky, why don't you help Tiana back downstairs with the breakfast tray? And take Troubles with you."

Nicklaus quickly scooped up the dirty dishes and loaded the rest of the breakfast things on the tray. "Come on, Tiana. Mom and Dad want to be alone."

"How do you know?" She wrapped her arms around the dog's neck, and Troubles gratefully licked the syrup off her face.

"I'm older than you, and I know these things."

Mariette called to her children as they crossed the threshold. "Keep things tidy down there. Your uncle Frank and aunt Carlotta are coming over later."

Looking back, Tiana tossed her locks and lifted her chin. "Is Corby coming too?"

"No, sweetheart. He's working."

Christian said, "Nicklaus, shut the door on your way out."

The boy nodded, closing the bedroom door.

"You know," Mariette said. "Corby might be the perfect person to run the shops while we go to Europe. Your nephew has all the quick-thinking inventiveness of his father."

Christian grabbed Mariette around the waist as she started to exit the bed. She continued talking as her husband pushed her back down, holding her wrists. "And the fortitude of Uncle Christian."

Christian never heard the words: "And the drop-dead good looks of the two of you." Mariette's mouth was too busy returning his impulsive kiss.